FISHBOWLS

and

BIRDCAGES

JENNIE CAMPBELL

©2015 Jennie Campbell

ISBN-13: 978-1511665476
ISBN-10:1511665475

For those preachers' wives out there
who have argued with God,
questioned God's call,
have done their best
to be the women they
were created to be,
and who understand what it's
like to live in a fishbowl or a birdcage.

And for Wade and Brian

TODAY

I'm sitting out on my open porch in my hammock swing, watching the puffy summer clouds of summer drift by above me, listening to the birds singing in the trees and to the wind making music as it passes through the pine needles of the little forest surrounding me. My wind chimes catch the breeze and add their voice to the afternoon's melody. I'm sipping on my afternoon glass of wine - Riesling, today. Memories are drifting past along with the clouds as I look back over my life and stop to wonder how I got here, to this place, and to this year.

I had my 65th birthday last week. A few friends and family were here in my country home to celebrate my eligibility for Medicare and to wish me bon voyage into an unknown future, that of official retirement. I only have a handful of what I consider good friends. A handful is enough – more than that and they become cumbersome and slip through my fingers and are gone. I like it this way. It's easier for me to keep track of who to care about and who will be here for me, should I need a shoulder to cry on or someone to share a pitcher of margaritas with. There were also a few of my great-nieces and nephews present to wish me a Happy Birthday. They think I'm cool, and like to come over whenever they have a chance to get a dose of Aunt Fran's funny ways and simple living. Gives them something to talk about with their friends at their next party.

I live in the small town of Wellspring, Georgia. Quaint sounding, isn't it? It's on the map, but you really have to know where it is and then put on your magnifying reading glasses to see it. Wellspring has one traffic light, one Methodist Church and one Baptist Church. That's about all you can say about the little town.

I've lived here for the past 17 years and have been a member of the Methodist Church since a few years after I bought my home on my 2 acres of pine forest two miles outside of town. If you were to drive into town looking for me, you probably wouldn't find anyone who knows who I am, or who cares. Possibly, you'd run into the local chiropractor (who's always out on the street drumming up business for her back-cracking profession) or the president of the Wellspring Historical Association, keeping a close eye on the town's antebellum homes, who'll say, "Frances McDougall? Isn't she the lady who lives in the old Thompson place out on Route 62? Don't see much of Miss Fran, but I can tell you where she lives. She doesn't come into town very often." I love the way every female in town over the age of thirty is automatically Miss Something or other. It's a southern thing.

So, here I sit, swinging and drinking on this sultry summer afternoon. My two gardens are growing nicely, the one that blesses me with vegetables all summer long, and the one that provides me with herbs to flavor my food and relieve my aches and pains. My life drifts before me and I realize it is time to share my story with someone. If I am known for anything, there are three things – the jellies I make and give away to anyone who shows the slightest interest in me, the cookies I bake at Christmas time, and the fact that I'm a preacher's ex-wife, a title that can make me or break me, according to who I share this small tidbit of information with. The latter is the story I have to share. Jelly and cookies make a pretty uninteresting tale.

Eccentric is the word I think most people would use to describe me, mostly people who don't know a thing about me. It's a pretty good word, but I don't want to be confined to this one description. I am much more than merely eccentric. I consider myself too complicated and complex for this simple label. However, I guess it's a good start for those who really don't know me and who only observe the little woman that they see as I make my way around the outskirts of Wellspring.

I only venture into town to pick up my mail at the post office a couple of days each week and sit in the same pew at the Methodist Church for the early service, maybe once a month if I'm in the mood. People might also catch a glimpse of me at the grocery store early on a weekday morning when I run out of staples or have the craving for some strawberry ice cream, and they might see me early in the morning when I go on my daily bicycle ride up and down our country roads or when I am walking my dog in the late afternoons.

To look at me, one might also label me a hermit, or an old hippie, but I'm not. I just enjoy my own company and that of my German Shepherd, Maggie, and my two cats of color, Martin and Coretta, who judge me by the content of my character and not by the color of my skin, more than that of the majority of the citizens of Wellspring.

My life is my own, and my history is, as well. I choose to share both only with those I believe will appreciate the tale and who might learn a little something that they can apply to their own lives.

Until this day, for the past 20 years, I've lived by the motto, "If you want to know, ask. If you don't, then don't bother me."

For too many years my life was one of circling in a fishbowl or perched in a birdcage, visible for everyone to observe and scrutinize and criticize. I had no private place, no room of my own, as Virginia Woolf put it so nicely. I was placed into a life that didn't fit me, and for many years this clothing that I wore chafed me and clung to me like an ill-fitting pair of thong underwear. If you've ever worn a thong, you know what I'm talking about.

The few people I still hang out with occasionally who have known me since childhood tell me that I haven't changed a bit.

Liars!

It irks me when they proclaim, "Fran, you're the same as you were when we were in high school. I'd know you anywhere!"

I think they are fishing for compliments for themselves. But then when I look at myself in the mirror, I can see an older version of the fifteen-year-old, as well, if I scrunch up my eyes and squint really hard. I guess I've become so accustomed to looking beneath the skin and past the face and smile, that I question their sincerity. So, maybe they could be right.

I now have white hair instead of brown. My eyes and face are creased with lines of laughter and tracks of tears, and my neck has more creases than an un-ironed cotton shirt. I'm twenty pounds heavier - and carry it nicely, thank you very much - and am a whole lot smarter. In many ways, perhaps I haven't changed. But this is why I have the desire to tell my story – not to show people that I'm the same person I've always been, but to expose myself as one who has peeled away the mask of trying to be who others expect me to be only to discover a person I never knew existed until my life was half over.

PART ONE

BEGINNINGS

Jennie Campbell

DREAMS AND DAYDREAMS

I always believed that I would grow up, have a beautiful wedding, settle down in a comfortable house somewhere with lovely flower beds lining the front walkway, and have a few children, in that order. As it turned out, the order that all of this happened wasn't as I had planned it, and the vision in my mind was far from what turned out to be reality.

When I was eighteen years old, I fell in love for the first time. Kyle asked me out for a school dance during my senior year of high school, and after dating for a few months, he abruptly dumped me with no explanation. One day he was waiting for me on the school breezeway to walk with me to my locker and on to homeroom, and the next day he was nowhere to be found. I didn't understand what I had done to make him lose interest in me.

I was heartbroken and immature enough to believe that love would never find me again. I spent the remainder of my senior year leaning and crying on

Kyle's best friend, Jeff's, shoulder, seeking affirmation and admiration. Jeff and I sang in the school chorus together, and were in the school drama group. He was a handy sounding board for my battered self-image.

"Why couldn't he break up with me to my face?" I begged Jeff for an explanation. "What did I do to make him not like me anymore?"

"He's a jerk," was Jeff's simple answer. "I don't think you did anything to him. He's just a coward. There's more behind this than you can see. Let it go, Fran, and forget about him."

Being Kyle's best friend, Jeff wouldn't elaborate about Kyle's actions, but I knew he was right - there had to be more than he was willing to tell me. I understood a little better a few weeks later when Kyle began dating a cute and popular cheerleader who was the daughter of one of the prominent lawyers in our town. Kyle's father was a doctor, making me believe that social status had a lot to do with it all, but I wondered if I were prettier or peppier he might not have broken up with me. It was hard for me to accept that it might have something to do with my father and what he did for a living, and not with me.

I didn't realize until years later the feelings Jeff had for me. He wanted to go out with me but wouldn't because of his loyalty to Kyle. Jeff was safe and non-demanding, and he became my crutch and confidante, and in actuality my best friend until we hugged goodbye the night of our graduation.

Jeff headed to Army basic training, and I began a summer job as a counselor at a youth community center. I didn't see or hear from him until our high school 10-year reunion when he showed up after being released from the Army and a tour of Vietnam. We sat and talked for hours while Kyle, still a bachelor, stood nearby getting drunk at the bar, never coming over to say hello to either of us. I watched with mixed emotions as Jeff took off from the reunion on his motorcycle, headed for parts unknown to heal. It's sad what Vietnam did to so many of its soldiers.

I met Chad, my second love and future husband, while working at the center, where he was finishing an internship for his college studies. I was still pining over Kyle, and very unsure about ever getting another boyfriend. Chad was charming, funny - and also insecure - but I didn't see this at the time. I clung to him with the vengeance of a drowning cat. On one hand I was still burned from my Kyle experience; on the other, I had a very juvenile notion that I was not complete as a person without a boyfriend. He was afraid of love for fear of being hurt, and I was afraid of being tossed aside and left alone again. We were the perfect couple. He was outgoing and entertaining; I was quiet and shy. Chad was a good-looking guy, and his sparkling blue eyes and a contagious smile melted my heart. He was always clean-shaven and well dressed, very attractive to anyone he met. The kids at the center loved him, and hung around him every chance they got. After we had begun getting to know each other, testing the waters to see if it was too cold to swim in the sea of our newfound attraction, he confessed to me that he had promised himself that he would only marry someone who was pretty. This statement, along with the one he made early on about being afraid of being hurt, set my mission in life. It wasn't until years later, when looking back, I could see and understand why he felt the way he did. It didn't matter to the 18-year-old me.

"Fran," he confessed after we had been dating only a few weeks. "I don't think I could stand it if you broke up with me. You are so pretty, and probably have lots of guys who want to go out with you. I just know that you'll find someone else and forget about me."

"Oh, Chad, I would never hurt you," I gushed, gazing into those blue eyes of his and squeezing his hands in mine. "You're too special to me. You don't have anything to worry about," I promised. "I'll always be here for you."

With this pledge, I was reassured that as long as we were together and he considered me to be pretty, I would love him and never hurt him, and I didn't have to worry anymore about being attractive enough for a man to notice me.

After the summer job ended, I left to go to college in another state, and he left to finish his senior year at his college, a state school. The next year was one of letter writing and weekly phone calls, with personal visits during school breaks mixed in.

The relationship was perfect for me. I had a boyfriend in another state, so I didn't feel pressured to date or even be nice to the boys I met on my campus. I hid behind the ghost of Chad for a year, not realizing that this was only a practice run for my place in his life for the next 20-odd years. I was young and needing reassurance that I was desirable. He was young and in search of someone who would keep him safe. Little did I know that this long-distance courtship would be the first of many ingredients in a recipe for a life I had no way to even imagine at the time.

The following year he graduated from college, and we got married, and indeed, it was a beautiful wedding, complete with white gown, bridesmaids, and loads of wedding gifts. I dropped out of college, and he got a teaching job in a small town, where we found a cute little apartment.

Let's see here. Grow up, get married, have a home, start a family. This was the order that things were supposed to happen in my vision of the perfect life. I certainly thought I was grown up, so I was on track. I didn't realize it then, and didn't for many years following, that I messed up the order. I wasn't grown up and wouldn't be until after we had been married for over two decades and I was going through the rituals of divorce. I was nineteen years old, but I considered myself mature and ready to face anything life had to toss my way. Looking back, I shudder as I think about how ill-prepared I was, but I also pat myself on the back for handling and dodging life's darts and arrows as well as I did.

The thought of Chad ever being a minister was the farthest thing from my mind – not even out there on my radar screen. He was a teacher and coach, and I was his cute little wife who graced his side at school functions and made him smile and puff up when his buddies would comment to him about my good looks. He'd tell me what they said, beaming with pride, and I would be happy, knowing that someone out there thought I was pretty.

The third item on my list for a happy life, a home of my own, was the next thing on my agenda. With Chad well established in the local school system, this seemed the likely next step from the apartment that was home for the first few years of our marriage.

Chad didn't want me to work. He liked the idea of being the family provider. In the 60s, more and more women were beginning to step out and have professions of their own in addition to husbands and families, but I wasn't one of them. The term *women's lib* was coming into vogue, but first we had to get past love beads, independent thinking, and a myriad of mind-altering drugs. The term was budding in the minds and lives of my female peers, many of whom found themselves in universities and sororities, with a handful turning their backs on all traditions to move to communes, live in tents, or otherwise terrify their parents.

I was too much my father's daughter, and my desire to make him happy took precedence over everything, except Chad. My father was disappointed that I didn't finish my college education before marriage, but in his mind a woman's education was only an insurance policy, "something to fall back on in case your husband dies." He considered nursing or teaching ideal courses of study, and my older sister already had her nursing degree, hating every minute of her hospital job while waiting for her Prince Charming to come rescue her on his gallant steed.

I promised my dad that I would return to school when we got settled, and he seemed satisfied, if not happy. Never one to take many risks, or to buck the system, I fell right into step with the wishes of Chad and my father. Staying at home, taking care of our three-room apartment, and cooking meals for my husband relieved me of any decision-making about my own future and personal needs. It didn't matter that we were poor, living paycheck to measly paycheck - it was important to Chad to be in charge of his little family and to have control over his tiny universe.

I thought I was fat. I was barely 5 feet tall and weighed a whopping 105 pounds. I also had complexion problems and almost always sported at least one big red zit somewhere on my face. My butt poked out further than I thought it should, and I was almost flat-chested. My hair was wavy and coarse - very unruly unless I kept it cut short and close to my head. Now, as I look back at photos of myself, I see a great little body, hard muscled from an active life, and free from excess fat anywhere. Funny how per-spectives change!

Chad never said anything about my figure, but he dropped hints on a regular basis that I needed to exercise more or become active in a sport of some kind. I ate little for breakfast, limited my lunch to a diet milkshake, and counted my calories for dinner. He kept count of the cookies that were in the cookie jar, and knew exactly how many he had eaten and how many more were missing from the jar. I thought he was being supportive, helping me to keep from "letting myself go." It also seemed that he was overly concerned about outward appearances, both mine and his. He worked out with weights, enjoyed sports of all kinds, and would have liked it if I had done the same.

My entire focus was on pleasing him and making him proud to have me by his side. Chad liked to show me off. He was proud of me and how I looked. Maybe it was that he wanted people to see that an ordinary guy like him could grab a beauty. It was a lot for me to live up to, but I took everything to heart and wanted more than anything to be loved and desired. At 20 years old, it wasn't a big deal for me, but it laid the foundation for how my life would be down the road.

On an intimate basis, those early days were a puzzle to me. Chad had a strong libido, and his need for sex was always tapping me on my shoulder. What I couldn't understand was our very different ideas about sex. For me, it was more emotional than physical. I wanted, more than anything, to be held close and cherished. For Chad, on the other hand, it was a strong physical urge, and seemed to have little to do with love or emotion. Being the virgin that I was when we married, I figured that this was the way all men were. I didn't understand it, but from the few conversations I had with my mother before I married about the woman's role in a marriage, I assumed that this was just the way things were. I believed Chad loved me, and was certain he needed me, but the sexual part of our relationship had me baffled, and left me wondering if I might be missing something or doing something wrong.

Chad needed me, but he also needed to be needed.

I didn't see the flashing warning signs.

PRETTY IS AS…

It's funny how my desire to be pretty for Chad led me by the nose through all my years with him. Even now, with long white hair that sometimes looks more like a wild snowstorm than a hairdo, and a face that never graces make-up of any kind, I want to be pretty. And I want heads to turn, which, except when attached to old men, they never do anymore.

Recently, while in the grocery store an elderly gentleman struck up a conversation with me, and would have taken me home with him had I been willing. Probably my own age, he seemed old, and in my mind I was still an alluring young woman. Some things never change. It's more of how we approach them that shapes us. As I talked to this kind man, I could imagine what he must have looked like as a younger version, and affirmed in my mind that as men age, they get better looking, while as women age, we only get old.

As reality set in, I wondered why he was so interested in me, until I remembered a wise older cousin's warning to me, "Men our age and older are looking for either a nurse or a purse."

Since it was in Walmart where I ran into this gentleman, I knew that I wasn't purse material and figured that a huge bank account probably didn't exist with him, either. And I certainly couldn't qualify as a nurse! Even though I spent over twenty years of my life taking care of Chad's fragile ego, I can now silently say, "I'm not interested" even though I have to admit I was flattered by the attention, and carried around an inner glow for a couple of days afterward.

I believe that I am still pretty, and I'm sticking with it.

THE CHURCH

Church was part of our life together from the beginning. Another of Chad's requirements in a wife was that she was a Christian and an active participant in church. I fit the mold somewhat, but was uneasy from the start whether I measured up in both Chad's eyes or in God's.

I had grown up in the Methodist Church, joining the church when I was eleven years old, and becoming active in the youth group when I reached high school age. I considered myself a Christian, but had never had what was called "a personal relationship with Christ" that was part of just about every sermon I ever heard. I had lots of unanswered questions about religion and faith, and wondered from time to time why I hadn't had an earth-moving experience to set my life on the road to salvation or felt the power of being born again.

I was simply a little girl who loved the music of the church and felt at peace sitting in a church pew gazing at the stained glass windows, and soaking in the beauty of the warm wood paneling, the strong beams, and the polished brass pipes of the organ. I often cried during the hymns, unable to sing them, they moved me so. I also liked the social aspect of church activities, and spent almost every Sunday evening at activities for whatever grade level I was in at the time, always part of the group, never the leader.

After we married, Chad and I joined the local Southern Evangelical Church and soon were involved in all kinds of church activities. Chad played on the men's softball team, I joined a ladies' daytime circle. We attended a couples' Sunday School class and church services on both Sunday morning and evening. The church sanctuary was a modern design and not warm and comforting like the one I grew up in. It didn't feel the same to me.

Chad loved playing softball and attending Sunday School class. I went with him to his softball games and sat with the other wives on the bleachers, never feeling like I fit in with them or having much to contribute to the ball game chit-chat or team cheering. I would watch the game, stand up and clap at the appropriate times, and wish for it to be over. Sunday School was the same. I was strictly an observer, and never felt comfortable or at ease among the other members of the class.

My uneasiness was the same with the ladies' circle. The only reason I joined was because Chad thought I'd make friends there and encouraged me to have activities to fill my days. All of the women were older than I was, and I had very little in common with them.

I felt like an outsider looking in and dreaded going each time the circle met. I especially hated the part of each program where we sat in a circle and each person had to say a sentence prayer. They all sounded phony to me, and also rehearsed. I didn't pay much attention to what prayers were being lifted to God, because I was sitting at my place in the circle breaking out in a sweat and panicking over what I would say when it was my turn – I was rehearsing, too. It may have been a meaningful prayer time for everyone else, but for me it was a tad below torture. I wondered what God thought about those prayers, and if he paid much attention to them at all. I didn't dare tell Chad how I felt about the ladies' circle, because he seemed so pleased that I was becoming active in the church, and he thought that I was enjoying it all.

I really did like church, primarily for the music, and for a small-town church, it did amazingly well in the music department. The organist was conservatory trained and taught music at a small college in a neighboring town. The choir was half-decent, its shortcomings drowned out by the talents of the organist. I loved getting to church early to listen to the prelude and bask in the sweet solitude of the sanctuary. I decided that if I were ever forced to choose which of my senses to lose, my eyesight or my hearing, it would definitely be the eyes that would have to go. I didn't think, and still don't, that I could survive without music.

One Sunday in Sunday School, Chad got upset with the person leading the lesson. He didn't agree with what was being taught, and didn't like the teacher questioning his ideas and thoughts. Chad was a talker and liked to add his opinions to whatever conversation or discussion was going on at the time. It made me nervous, and I began to tense up just knowing that Chad was about to get into an argument. I was a passive person, and a peacemaker. I was, and still am, uncomfortable amid conflict, and want to fix things in order to bring my world back into equilibrium. I am also introverted and non-confrontational. When the Sunday School bell rang, Chad silently stalked out of the classroom with me on his heels, smiling at everyone and making small talk to reassure them and myself that everything was OK. All during the church service I could feel the tension building sitting next to me in the person of my husband.

Nothing more was said until later that week when Chad announced to me at dinner, "I talked to Rev. Williams today and offered to begin a new Sunday School class for young adult couples. I volunteered for the two of us to be team teachers of the class. It begins this Sunday."

"You did what?" I questioned. "Why didn't you talk me about this first? I've gotten used to the class that we're in. I don't want to leave it."

"Fran, this is a chance for me to take on a leadership role in the church, and I really need you to back me up and help me. I'm counting on you to help make this work for us."

Chad went on to tell me that he'd lead the class and I would be his helper to keep discussions going and to recruit members. He also thought that some of the couples in the class we were attending might come with us to help start the new class. I don't know why Rev. Williams went along with Chad's idea so readily, but then Chad could be very convincing when there was something that he wanted.

I wasn't as confident as Chad was. "What about the class we're in? Won't they be upset with us for jumping ship?" I asked. "What will they think of us if we steal members away from the class?"

"Don't worry about it, Fran," Chad reassured me. "Rev. Williams agrees that the church is ready for a new class, and we're the perfect couple to get it started. This is God's will – I'm sure of it. It's all gonna be fine."

I wasn't excited about leading a class or having to go out to talk to people to invite them to join. Chad was very convincing that this was something he felt that God wanted him to do, so who was I to question God? If this was God's will, then everything would be OK, I reasoned to myself. I didn't voice any further my hesitation to Chad, but went along with him and supported him in his plans.

The next Sunday found us sitting in the pastor's office, the only place available for our new class. One other couple joined us, the only dropouts from the other class, and we were off and running. All of my fears about upsetting people were unfounded – at least as far as I ever heard. Those who stayed in the other class were probably very happy to see us go!

It turned out that Chad was a dynamic teacher, and it wasn't long before our little group had grown to several couples, mostly those who hadn't been involved in Sunday School, or who were new to the church.

Every Sunday I sat quietly in my seat, and listened to the lesson and the discussion. I seldom contributed to the class, or had much to say. I didn't always agree with what was being taught or discussed, but I was too shy and unsure of myself to speak out and ask questions or state an opinion. Chad was in his glory every Sunday. He'd study his lesson for several hours on Saturday night, make notes, and prepare for class. He wanted his lesson to be perfect.

It paid off, and before long our class was one of the largest ones in the church. I was always being told what a wonderful teacher my husband was. I was very proud of him, and loved that he was getting all of the praise for helping the church grow and prosper.

The only problem - and I didn't see it then - was that I was beginning to disappear from view behind him. I had very little identity of my own, and it was fading in his shadow. The foundation for our future was being laid at this little church, but I didn't know it during those first few years of our marriage. I was too absorbed in my own insecurity and in my happiness of being married to such a popular and outgoing guy.

In later years I commented to a close friend that I felt like I was invisible.

Life in our small town moved quietly forward with the passing of time. We had been married two years when I learned that I was pregnant. We were still living in our little one-bedroom apartment – no house yet – and we weren't financially ready for either a house or a baby. That didn't matter to me. I was delighted. Chad was also pleased, but I knew that he was worried about how we would manage. His job was beginning to bore him, and he had been talking about making a change before my announcement that we were going to be parents. He was also somewhat perturbed with me for letting this happen when we weren't planning for it.

The truth was that I was on a mechanical form of birth control – a cream very popular at the time. This was before the birth control pill was widely accepted, and taking it carried a lot of side effects and dangers that I didn't want to deal with. The cream worked pretty well if you used it according to the directions. The night I got pregnant the container and applicator never left the drawer of my bedside table. This was the night that Chad decided that it was time for me to get drunk for the first time in my life.

FIGURING THINGS OUT

My two sons, Kent and Dan were at my 65th birthday party. Kent, the more blunt of the two, and the younger, asked me, "Mom, how do you feel about being 65 years old?"

I looked at him square in the eyes and said, "It doesn't bother me nearly as much as seeing you turn 40."

That's the truth, too. My own age means nothing to me. I live each day as if it's my last, while planning to live forever. It's a good way to face each morning, and keeps both me and my brain active. I don't like watching my sons grow older, though, and to think of them as middle-aged men is beyond my comprehension. They are, and always will be, my little boys. I know neither of my sons likes the idea of my getting old any more than I like seeing them age.

Ever since they were babies, we had such great times together and were very close. I was in my 20s when they were both born, very mature and grown up - or so I thought - but still very much a child.

I had a motto that if there was something fun to do with my kids, the house could wait. And it did. Many, many times. Ultimately, we lived in a cluttered house most of the time, with dishes piled up in the sink, a mountain of unfolded clothes on one of the beds or the sofa, and a carpet begging to be vacuumed. Not a desired state of affairs for parsonage living, that's for sure! We still laugh about it and remember how it drove Chad crazy, being the neatnik that he was and the lover of clear surfaces and order in his environment.

The boys and I carry on whenever we get together and are children - me included - again. I am thankful that they picked up on my philosophy about having fun in life. Although we are all three pretty good housekeepers these days, we'll drop everything in the blink of an eye if something more interesting beckons us.

When I think back to that day when I found out I was pregnant, I knew my life was changed forever, but I didn't have a clue as to what it would be like to be a mother and to have a child to care for. Chad was worried about being a father and having a family; I was in my element, my dream was coming true, and I didn't ever think twice about the future, how we'd take care of a child or what might change when there were three of us, not two.

In many ways, having Kent and Dan saved my life. They gave me so much joy, I cannot fathom what life would have been without them. In a life that kept taking sharp turns with little or no warning, having my boys close to me gave me stability and an anchor. Chad's life was his own, and even though I was married to him, and the boys were his children, he lived his life for himself – we were merely passengers along for the ride. Whatever he decided to do, we all did. It never really mattered how we felt.

Now, looking back, I see things so clearly. I'm not much of a Biblical scholar, but I understand Paul writing about looking through a glass dimly, and then face to face. Of course he was talking about his relationship with Jesus, while in my case it's my own life that I see more clearly now, looking face to face at myself. While I've never gotten toilet-seat-hugging drunk again, I look back at that night and see very clearly how it molded my life from that moment forward.

We have many times like that in our lives where events that seemed insignificant at the time play a major role in our life story. Would I go back and change something from my life? If I could, would I be happy with the results?

I wonder.

A few years before I retired I had the privilege of taking the Myers-Briggs personality inventory test. My employer, in an attempt to improve productivity, decided that this would be a good way for us to examine our strengths and weaknesses and to determine if we were in the right job, or if we might need to make a change or adapt our work to our personality profile. It was an eye-opener for me. For the first time, I realized how very different Chad and I were, and how our marriage was destined for turbulence, if not disaster. It also brought light onto all of the uncomfortable times I had in that Sunday School class, and all those that followed, and why I felt like an outsider at the church activities.

I sit here swinging on my porch swing today, with most of my life behind me, and in reminiscing the many paths my life took and how I maneuvered along the way, I wish I had known then what I know now. It might not have been any easier, but at least I would have understood things better, and possibly would have coped more easily.

I sit and swing, and enjoy my solitude. My head is swimming with words that I want to write and stories I need to tell. I'll go out to my garden later to weed and take care of my vegetables, and I'll check my herbs to make sure everything there is growing and thriving.

I am alone today, but certainly not lonely.

BEING PREGNANT

Because I was in love with Chad during my freshman year in college, I never took part in the party life at my school. I spent most Friday and Saturday nights in the dorm writing letters to Chad, working on my class assignments and listening to music on my stereo. My two roommates were party girls, and many weekends they would come home from a fraternity party drunk as skunks. In a way I envied them for their free-spirited lives, and I often wondered what it felt like to be high, happy, and uninhibited. The following morning, however, I was glad that I hadn't been where they had the night before, because they had terrible hangovers. It was also illegal for girls our age to drink, and as a rule-follower, I used this as one of my many excuses for not joining them. So it was that I got through my freshman year in college without experiencing the effects of alcohol.

After Chad and I got married, he wanted me to drink with him. We couldn't afford much alcohol, but on occasion we'd buy a bottle of wine, or some rum to add to our Cokes. I never drank more than one glass at a sitting. It was on this fateful Saturday night that

Chad convinced me that it was time for me to learn what it felt like to be drunk. He promised to take care of me and not let anything terrible happen to me. I don't know what I thought might happen, but the thought of losing control of my senses and my will terrified me.

We started with rum and cokes and moved on to vodka and orange juice. Never should have done the OJ on top of the other drinks. I began to feel dizzy and then disoriented. Once I was good and drunk, Chad, who was also showing the effects of our drinking party, was ready to have sex, and I wasn't in any shape to even think about the birth control in the bedside table drawer.

I don't remember feeling much during the time we were together, and wondered what the big deal was about getting drunk. I thought alcohol was supposed to enhance sex. As soon as the deed was done, my stomach started churning – I was getting sick and soon to be sicker.

The next hour I hugged the toilet bowl while Chad sat on the tub behind me wiping my forehead with a damp rag and assuring me that I'd live. When my insides were finally empty, I vowed never to get drunk like that again, and hated Chad for wanting me to experience it. He thought it was all very funny – that is until he found out that I had gotten pregnant that night.

I learned that I was pregnant after I had missed two periods. In those days, before at-home pregnancy tests, all we had to rely on was our own bodies and what they were doing for us and to us. My doctor confirmed tentatively, by examination, that he was pretty sure I was pregnant, but it took a urine test and another three days for the phone call to arrive that indeed I was expecting a baby, or as my doctor so gently informed me, "Fran, you have a turkey in the oven."

"A what?" I asked him over the phone, and innocently added, "I'm not cooking anything right now."

Laughing, he explained, "Fran, you're pregnant. You're going to have a baby in about seven months."

Love those small Southern town doctors!

I was already beginning to feel the queasiness of morning sickness, which wasn't nearly as bad as my experience with being drunk a couple of months earlier. I thought at first it was my imagination and that my period would arrive any day now. The doctor's confirmation set my heart on the next seven months, and I was eager to begin wearing maternity clothes and get ready for baby.

While excited about the baby, I was also very sleepy most of the time, and fell asleep on the sofa every evening after supper. Chad didn't like this much. He wanted me to sit with him and watch "our" favorite television shows until bedtime, when he was ready to go to bed and make love. My doctor had assured me that having sex wouldn't hurt me or my baby, which disappointed me to a certain degree. I was hoping for a reprieve for awhile. I still hadn't figured out what the big hubbub was about sex. It didn't do a thing for me, and I put up with Chad's nightly needs because I loved him and wanted to make him happy. I was hoping that pregnancy would slow him down a bit, but it didn't. I think it actually took away the fear of making me pregnant for him, which since I was already that way, he didn't have to worry about it for awhile.

After the initial shock, Chad began crowing like a rooster about his success in the hen house. I wasn't eager to tell everyone yet, but it wasn't a week before everyone in the church and his school knew that we were expecting a baby. I told my parents as soon as I found out, and was relieved that they were happy for me, even though this meant that I'd be putting off keeping my promise to Daddy to return to school and get my degree. They sent me money for the baby's crib, and my mom began piecing a quilt for the little one - of course it would have both pink and blue in it, since we didn't know whether baby would be a boy or a girl. How I envy those young mothers now who know ahead of time the sex of their baby, so that they can select the name and pick out appropriate baby clothes ahead of time.

Life was good for the next few months. I could feel the butterfly wings of the baby's first movements after another couple of months, and my tummy began to bulge, making it hard to fasten my regular clothes. The morning sickness lessened and I had more energy. But then I began having slight spotting and a nagging backache that was new. My doctor told me to walk at least a mile each day, watch my diet, get plenty of rest, and everything would be fine.

It wasn't.

One night after making love – Chad was insistent that if the doctor said I was okay, then it would be just fine for us to have sex - the backache became worse until I could hardly bear it to stand up. I called my doctor, and he told us to meet him at the hospital immediately. Chad went bonkers. He was running around the apartment, not knowing what to do while I collected the car keys, our insurance card, made sure all of the appliances were turned off, and walked calmly to the car. I drove, while Chad fidgeted. Soon after I was admitted, things started happening pretty rapidly, and before I knew it, I wasn't pregnant anymore.

My body was empty, and I felt like a total failure. No women in my family had ever lost a baby. I must have done something wrong to make this happen. There was no funeral, no closure. After a day in the hospital, I was sent home and that was it. I never saw my baby or had the chance to say good-bye to him. It was as if nothing had happened, except that I was no longer pregnant. The guilt was unbearable, and depression set in, relieving the pain in sleep, only to waken from a nightmare about killing babies.

Chad was little help. He was sad, of course - the baby had been a boy – but he was also relieved. He kept telling me that it was God's will for this to happen.

Nonsense! I wasn't buying this copout, and refused to place God in a position of taking my unborn baby because of some cosmic will of his. I didn't know why this had happened to me, and I became angry at both God and Chad. It was this anger that brought me out of the depression, but it didn't do a thing for the guilt.

I truly believed that I had killed my baby. I wasn't sure how, whether it was the excessive walking, or the frequent sex that Chad required, but I could not be convinced that things like this just happen, and I certainly couldn't believe that they happen for a reason. My doctor assured me that the baby had been normal as far as he could tell, and he brushed it off as a spontaneous abortion, telling me that I'd have the opportunity to have another baby. I didn't want another baby; I wanted the one that was no longer growing in me.

Chad didn't know how to comfort me, and whatever he tried, failed. He kept reminding me that it was God's will, and inwardly I began to hate that phrase. He seemed relieved that it was just the two of us again and that I didn't have this baby stuff on my mind all the time. He chose the path of ignoring it and pretending that nothing had happened.

It certainly didn't affect him the same as it did me, and I couldn't understand why he seemed so cavalier about the entire episode. It was like a television show that he had watched and simply changed the channel when things became too uncomfortable for him to watch anymore. After taking a couple of days off from work, Chad was back at school as if nothing happened, and I was at home alone to face my personal demons.

It was during these days of healing that I began thinking about getting pregnant again. I had nothing enjoyable to do during the long days while Chad was at school, and I was bored. I thought that having a baby to care for would fill my days as well as the hole in my heart. I didn't know how to bring up the subject to Chad, so after a few months, when my doctor proclaimed me fully recovered, I began to scheme. I certainly wasn't going to go the route of getting drunk – I never wanted to repeat that night – and Chad was always very conscientious about the birth control, since it appeared that I was quite fertile.

I had never tried seduction – of any kind with anyone. With Chad's need for frequent sex, something like this had never even crossed my mind. Even foreplay was something foreign to me - he was so intense, I never had time to warm up, much less get hot. I often felt like Chad loved his penis more than he did me. I merely provided a handy place to put it. Sex for him seemed to be purely physical, with little or no emotion attached.

Building on this idea, I decided to give a little seduction a try, but wasn't sure how to go about it, having never had any practice. One Friday afternoon, an idea formed in my mind as I showered. I got out of the shower, put on perfume and a slinky negligee from my trousseau, and applied eye shadow, liner and mascara, and bright red lipstick.

Then I waited.

When Chad walked through the door, I was waiting for him, looking as sexy and provocative as I could. Upon seeing my image, he responded immediately, began shedding his clothes, and before either of us knew it, we were on the bed making love. I felt like a whore, seeing how he responded to the vision I presented and the way he forgot everything else in order to get on top of me and inside of me. I didn't feel like myself, but seemed like someone I didn't know, and didn't like very much. Not a great experience for me, but that was the day that Dan was conceived, so the charade was worth it, as far as I was concerned.

I was thrilled to learn that I was again pregnant, even though I kept thinking back to that day, feeling conflicted – it had felt like an affair, or possibly even a rape. Chad was very forceful with me, and there was no feeling of intimacy, only pressure and pain. His weight on me was suffocating. It really felt like I had been taken, and not made love to. I was relieved when it was over and I could wash my face and put on clean clothes.

Afterward, I never asked Chad about it, but then he never mentioned it to me or asked me to dress up that way ever again. It planted a seed of doubt in me, though. I was never sure what he was thinking about during my little charade, and I think it also put a knick in his trust in me to be faithful to him. After that day, even before I knew that I had become pregnant again, our relationship was a little different than before, at least from my perspective, and based on future clashes between the two of us, from his as well.

This pregnancy was uneventful, and I felt wonderful the entire nine months. Dan was born following an easy labor - as far as labors go - and I had my beautiful, perfect son in my arms. I breastfed him, and savored the hours that I held him in my arms and at my breast. Chad took second chair to Danny and watched us from a distance. He loved his little boy, but wasn't comfortable holding him or caring for him, and didn't have a lot to do with him until he was almost a year old and learning to walk. New routines took the place of the old ones where there were only the two of us, and my life was filled with motherhood and all it entailed.

Chad continued with his teaching job and with all of his church activities, which were growing. He took on more leadership roles, began to sing in the choir - even though he was tone deaf - and became intensely interested in religion. His paying job began to take a lesser role for him, and he began hinting that he might want to make a career change.

By the next year, I was pregnant again, this time a surprise for both of us as we were very diligent with our birth control regime, and we welcomed the idea of a little brother or sister for Danny. Danny was an active and happy toddler. I was trying to figure out how to squeeze four of us into our little apartment, and I didn't have time in my day to contemplate what a new career might mean to us. I chose to listen to Chad talk about doing something different with his life, and promptly put these conversations aside to take the Scarlett O'Hara tactic - I'd think about it tomorrow.

Kent entered the world two years after his big brother, Dan. Another healthy boy, and although I had secretly wished and prayed for a little girl, God answered my prayer by giving Dan a little brother. Once I held him in my arms, all thoughts of pink lace and curly locks evaporated, and I was in love. Chad was happy, too, but like me, he had wanted to have a daughter. Dan was delighted and loved Kent from the first time he saw him.

I couldn't have asked for more. I still thought about my first baby, and wondered what life would have been like if he had been born, but these two little boys helped lessen the guilt that still plagued me, and my energy was now focused on my family squeezed into our tiny apartment, and not the little boy who might have been.

MY THOUGHTS, AGAIN

Dan and Kent are now adults and sliding rapidly through middle age. I look at them and know that I did something right. They are both attentive sons, while not hovering. I feel sure that they wish I didn't live alone, because then they wouldn't have to worry about me as much. I am very happy that they don't live in the same town as I do. I like my independence, and they like theirs. They are both city dwellers and love the urban life. They go through a severe case of culture shock whenever they come to visit me in Wellspring.

"Geez, Mom, you mean we have to drive ten miles to go to the grocery store?" Followed by, "What are you going to do when you can't drive anymore?"

"Why, I'll move in with one of you guys," I laugh. "You know your main job in life is to support your mother in her old age," I kid them.

Honestly, I'm not ready to think about that yet. I know the time will come when I have to face the facts that I am old, but for now I am healthy and happy, and don't want to be anywhere else on earth.

Neither of my sons is married. Dan tried it for a few years, but it didn't work out. Kent is a confirmed bachelor, surrounded by friends, but not interested in a permanent commitment. Sometimes I think they absorbed a little too much from their lives with their dad and me. Their growing up years were tough, with uprooting every few years and always being in the spotlight wherever we lived.

Each of my boys took different paths in adulthood. Dan lives in a sparsely furnished studio apartment for the time being, but is ready at a moment's notice to pack up and move. Kent has nested and has been in the same place for 15 years. I don't think you could pry him out of his home!

I am amazed that as adults they are relatively normal and both are successful in their chosen professions. Neither followed in their father's footsteps, as either teacher or preacher. Dan ended up being a museum archivist, and Kent wound up as a program director for a not-for-profit organization.

THE CALLING

During the first days after coming home from the hospital with Kent, I stayed pretty close to home. Chad spent a lot of time at the church, and almost every week-night he'd leave soon after supper to attend a meeting, choir practice, softball practice, or some other church activity. It was lonely for me, but I had my two little guys, and we became a team. We had our evening routine, which included bath time, nursing Kent until he fell asleep, and then reading stories and singing songs with Dan until he drifted off.

I was usually asleep, as well, when Chad would get home. He'd wake me up for sex, and then promptly fall asleep, while I lay awake after being roused from my rest. Soon after Kent had been born, Chad had a vasectomy, and while I wasn't in complete agreement with his decision, I signed the spousal consent, and it was done. The fear of pregnancy was no longer an issue, and Chad seemed to desire sex more than ever. If I begged off, pretended not to wake up when he got into bed, or didn't feel up to it, I'd see the bathroom light on late in the night where he'd be taking care of his needs in private. Because of my limited experience with men, I didn't see this as anything to be of concern. I assumed that all men were like Chad. And my mother had never told me anything about this male practice. I wasn't about to ask her now.

The conversations about a career change began to increase in frequency. Chad was not happy with teaching, and had problems with some of the other teachers, being very critical of them and the way they taught and dealt with the students. He always felt that his way was the only way and the right way. He was itching for a change of some kind.

We finally made the move to a small house when Kent was almost a year old, and with the new responsibility of a monthly mortgage payment, I was less than enthusiastic about Chad quitting his job to do something different. My plan for a happy life was proceeding, not exactly as I had planned, but things were looking pretty good and secure as I saw them.

One Sunday while Chad was at church and I was at home with the boys, I was watching an evangelist on television during the church hour. His message was one that I couldn't forget – *Bloom Where You Are Planted.* I took this message to heart, and saw myself as blooming in my little home, with my little family, and living happily ever after. This theme would later come to haunt me, as I rebelled against the preacher's advice in his sermon, not so much about blooming, but about being planted somewhere that I didn't want to be. This sermon was a forewarning for me, and in the events that were soon to come about, I often thought about this statement.

Among the many church activities that occupied Chad's time and energy was a Friday morning men's prayer breakfast that he attended faithfully every week. He'd leave the house around 5:30 am to meet the small group of men from the church at 6:00. They'd have breakfast together at a local restaurant, then pray or talk, or do whatever men do at a prayer breakfast, and then go to their respective jobs. On Fridays, I wouldn't see Chad until after school, since he left before I woke up.

One winter Friday morning, Chad gave me a quick kiss good-bye as he got out of bed and left to go to his prayer breakfast, and from there to work. A few minutes later I climbed out of the warmth of the bed and padded to the kitchen in my fuzzy slippers and fixed myself a cup of coffee to enjoy in the hour before Dan and Kent awakened to the new day.

It was very peaceful and still in the house that morning, with two sleeping little boys in their bedroom and the television still silent from its night's rest. I felt very content, and savored the alone time that was my Friday treat when Chad wasn't around for breakfast. I curled up on the easy chair with my coffee, tucked my feet up underneath my fleece robe, and let my thoughts wander. Time evaporated, and before I knew it, Dan was climbing up onto my lap, and Kent was making noises from his crib to let me know he had a wet diaper and was getting hungry.

The routines of the day began in earnest as I got the baby cleaned up and into his highchair at the dinette table and fixed Dan a bowl of Cheerios. I poured a handful of Cheerios onto Kent's tray. We were all happily eating our breakfast, when the reverie was interrupted by the back door opening and Chad walking through.

"What are you doing home? Is something wrong? Are you OK?" My mind was racing trying to figure out why he'd come back home instead of going to school.

"Everything is great, Fran!" he answered. "I have some great news to tell you." He was beaming with whatever secret he had for me.

Before I could come up with a question about what kind of exciting news was coming my way, Chad announced, "I've decided to go into the ministry. I'm going to be a preacher."

As I attempted to gather my wits, which had plopped onto the floor among the Cheerios Kent had wiped off his tray, Chad told me that he would be quitting his job, we were going to put our house up for sale, and that he was applying at a nearby seminary for divinity school. Rev. Williams was already on top of things and was making arrangements for Chad to take over a small church to minister while he attended school.

My whole world changed suddenly in the span of two hours.

Flabbergasted, I didn't know what to say or do. My stomach felt like it had been hit with a medicine ball, and my head was spinning. I couldn't take it all in, and didn't want to. This was more than I had in mind when I resolved to bloom where I was planted! I had just been ripped out of my flower pot, and if I was blooming, I didn't know anymore where I was planted! Chad reassured me that this was God's calling, that he had heard God's voice and had answered the call. Funny, God didn't call me or tell me that he was getting in touch with Chad. It seemed to me that He would let me in on this little secret before yanking me up from my home and security.

BLOOMING, GROWING, OR WILTING

Bloom where you are planted. Sometimes I wish I'd never heard that tacky sermon. It was the bane of my existence for years. Looking back at the young woman I was on that cold wintry day, I cry for her, and wish I could step back and give her peace of mind as well as a piece of my mind. Lousy advice for this shy young introvert – *bloom where you are planted.* It took me a long time to figure that one out.

I think I'd be more apt to advise her to "grow a backbone, and become strong. If, while you are doing this, you can bloom, then you're the woman I think you can become. Believe in blossoms without pots. Plant yourself in your own strength and within your own heart – don't ever settle for less simply because you are 'planted' in a particular spot on earth or with a husband who is a minister."

It's funny how I've become so much smarter since I've gotten old.

As I look back at myself as a young mother, with little real knowledge of life, I wonder how my life's path might have changed if I'd asked more questions, asserted myself more strongly, hadn't been convinced to believe that I couldn't confront either my husband or God about this major decision that was going to affect our entire family. There's no way of knowing how things would have been different, or if I'd even be here sitting in my hammock swing today telling this story. Or would it be another swing somewhere else, with a very different story?

It's at times like this, when I try too hard to analyze my life and create alternate realities for my past, that I push my hammock into a spin, and get dizzy as it goes round and round. The past won't change, no matter how much I might wish it could, and if I really pause to think about it, I'm not sure if I'd want it to change. I am the person I am today because of the young woman I was then, and I can honestly look at her, however, with empathy and understanding and say *thank you* to her.

TRANSITION

Soon after Chad made his announcement about going into the ministry, I found myself in a dizzying spiral of a new life I was totally unfamiliar with. Joan Williams, our minister's wife, who was a very nice woman in her mid 30's, took it upon herself to groom me for the life I was now entering.

"Fran, you're gonna make a great preacher's wife," she proclaimed to me one morning over tea in our kitchen.

I forced a smile, sipped my tea and questioned, "Do you really think so?"

But inside I was screaming, "What if I don't want to be a great preacher's wife? Why can't I be a great teacher's wife? Why is this happening to ME? I don't know if I can do this! I don't want to do this!"

"I know you will," Joan assured me. "You're a wonderful helpmate for Chad, and you are God's choice for him. You and he are a terrific team, and he's lucky to have you as his wife."

Joan meant well, but in reality she scared me to death, and the term *helpmate* was one that immediately sent shivers down my spine. Her stories of life in the parsonage, meant to make me feel more comfortable about selling my home and furniture, only made me resentful of the church. And, while I wasn't brave enough to be mad at God at that point, I was beginning to have ill feelings about him, too.

Joan told me about her husband's calling into the ministry and how happy she was that God had called her to be his life's partner and support in his ministry. It was hard enough for me to simply be in Sunday School class and participate in Bible discussions. I didn't know how I was going to be able to live up to the expectations of being a minister's wife. And I didn't fully grasp the term *helpmate*. I certainly didn't feel like I had helped my mate in this new plan. I decided that it was a term I really didn't like at all.

Joan laughed at what seemed to be an inside joke, and then told me that she was one of the lucky ones – she didn't know how to play the piano.

"You don't play, do you?" she asked, looking around from her perch at the kitchen bar, as if she were searching for one.

It was an old southern prerequisite that the preacher's wife had to know how to play the piano. She laughed that she got out of a lot of jobs simply because she had never taken piano lessons. While we didn't have a piano in our house, I determined then and there that nobody would ever know that I had taken seven years of piano lessons as a child, and I could play pretty well. My downfall was that I didn't let Chad in on this tidbit from Joan, and he let it slip in a conversation a few months later with his new pastor-parish committee that I indeed was a pianist. I could have shot him then and there.

I also didn't understand God's calling. I didn't doubt that Chad believed God had called him into the ministry, but I wasn't able to accept it then, and never could, that God had neglected to call me, as well, or at least let me in on his plan for Chad's life. It didn't seem fair. At times I felt like both God and Chad were ganging up against me.

During those early days when things were happening so fast for Chad and his calling, I spent a lot of time praying for God to give me a sign, talk to me, anything, that would reassure me that this was really happening and wasn't some kind of a dream or delusion.

I think it would have been different for me if I'd known about this from the beginning, if I'd fallen in love with a minister. But I didn't. The man I had fallen in love with had been a coach and a teacher, and he was now gone, replaced by someone I recognized by sight, but wasn't sure I knew. I tried talking to my parents about my misgivings, but they were so pleased with Chad's decision, I didn't get very far with them. Like Joan, they believed that I would make a wonderful minister's wife.

Chad's parents, on the other hand, thought he was crazy. Chad's dad looked at everything in life with dollar signs attached. He believed his son was throwing away a chance at a successful career for this pipe dream. Chad's mother was very proud of her son, but didn't risk crossing her husband to express any of her personal opinions or thoughts.

I had no one to pour out my heart to or anyone to listen to me and my misgivings. I kept running into brick walls of people who couldn't understand why I would have any misgivings whatsoever. It seemed that the entire world was thrilled with Chad's decision.

During the final months of winter and the early days of spring, my days were filled with doing things I never would have dreamed I'd be doing a few months earlier. I was completely uprooted from the place where I was planted, and I had no road map to follow for the path I was now traveling.

Our house now had a *For Sale* sign out front, and from time to time, a real estate agent would call, asking me and the boys to leave the house for awhile so that she could show it to a potential buyer. One day, she phoned to ask if she could show the house – in ten minutes. Kent was taking a nap, and I told her I wasn't going anywhere until he waked up.

A young couple, eager to purchase their first home, wanted to see it immediately, regardless of whether I was home. Accompanied by the real estate agent as they walked from room to room, opening my closets and kitchen cabinets, and critiquing my home, I could tell that they were interested. In a courteous gesture for invading my privacy with my little family, the young woman paused to admire Kent, still asleep in his crib, and whispered that the agent had told her that my husband was a preacher. Inwardly I recoiled. She then asked me a very pointed question, "I guess you're a religious person, aren't you?"

You'd think she had screamed this question in my ear. It was one I'd never been asked, and I had never thought too much about it. "Yes, I guess I am," I stammered. The words came out, but I wasn't sure if I believed them or if she heard them. I wonder if she did.

AM I RELIGIOUS, OR WHAT?

So, at 65 years of age, am I a religious person? I am amazed at how many times I have been asked this same question. I get a kick out of it, especially when it comes from someone who knows me simply as Fran McDougall, without my past draped around my shoulders. When I was in the workforce, those around me occasionally heard me let out a curse word, and my dress code certainly didn't hint that I had once lived within the confines of the church community. In the South, especially the rural South, certain expectations still pervaded about ministers' wives when I was young, and I certainly didn't fit the perceived mold.

I think about my answer to the question, knowing that it will come again, and wanting to answer it honestly while not leaving the impression that I have abandoned my faith. I continue to pester God, and at times question whether I am a Christian, although I believe that deep down inside I am. I have studied the Bible as well as history, and my Christian belief outgrew the Bible decades ago. I think of myself as being more spiritual than religious. I cringe at some of the things that come out of the local Methodist pulpit, and shudder at some of the behaviors I see from devout church members. However, I nurture my relationship with the holy spirit and feel God's presence in my life as the breath of all life. Yes, I am definitely spiritual, but I don't think of myself as being particularly religious.

Living alone, and with my handful of friends who respect my privacy, I spend a lot of my time in solitude. I have become keenly aware of the world around me and notice things like clouds, dirt, wild flowers, the color of the sky, the feel of the wind. I spend a great deal of time in conversation with God and feel his spirit surrounding me. At night, I look at the star-studded sky and know that God exists. You can explain the Big Bang Theory out the ying-yang to me, and I will always come back to one question, which has never been answered to my satisfaction by science: *what about origin?* For me, this is the question of the ages.

I see my life as an eternity sandwich. I am stuck right now between two eternities – the one before I was born and the one that follows my life. I imagine my second eternity as one in which I will be able to explore the universe, with no constraints on time or space. It sends shivers through my body when I try to embrace this thought, so I choose to concentrate on today, and let eternity take care of itself.

It took a long time for me to come to this sense of peace about my place in God's creation, and the church didn't help me in this journey.

MOVING INTO THE CHURCH WORLD

We ran an ad in the local newspaper to sell our furniture. Parsonages were fully furnished, so we had to get rid of all that we had accumulated. Chad was ready to sell everything. I put my foot down and refused to sell a pecan coffee table that my parents had given us for a wedding gift and the child's wardrobe I'd had since Dan was a baby. Other than those two items, and the baby crib, everything eventually exited our home, and each time someone bought something, I cried.

Chad, on the other hand, seemed to revel in all of this. One to like order and simplicity, it seemed that the emptier the house got, the better he liked it. He didn't want to move much to our new parsonage home, and encouraged me to sell or give away almost everything we had that wouldn't be needed where we were going. I refused to let go of our wedding gifts – the china, crystal, sterling flatware, silver-plated trays, all pretty much useless stuff in Chad's eyes. These things were special to me, even though we seldom used them.

Besides all of this going on around me, there were money problems. I knew we had them, but Chad kept all of the financial matters of our marriage from me. When I questioned him how we were going to pay for three years of theology school, he told me there was no need to worry, that he had everything figured out. I wasn't sure what he meant, but I trusted him, and since God had called him to the ministry, then maybe he and God had some kind of arrangement worked out. With our two children, I was living on a pretty tight budget, but somehow I managed to get by on what Chad gave me each month.

I was too consumed with all of the bits and pieces of packing up and getting ready to move that I put all of this in the back of my mind for the time being and became a passenger on this ride to a new life.

Chad had no qualms about his decision. He finished the school year, resigned his teaching position, and prepared for his new life behind the pulpit. He was as happy as I'd ever seen him, and he was anxious to move and set up shop in his own church. It seemed to me that he never considered me or the boys or how we were feeling about all of this. I concentrated on blooming where I was planted, and did my best to put forth a brave face on what we were doing, but inside I was a mishmash of confused feelings, unidentified fears, and latent animosity toward God, the church, and Chad, all rolled up into one festering infection.

In addition, I felt like I was adrift in an unknown ocean. All of my conversations with Joan had not had the results she meant for them to have. In her efforts to prepare me for becoming a preacher's wife, her main success was to instill more doubt and fear in me and to make me question myself even more than I had before all of this happened.

I didn't want to be a minister's wife, and I didn't want to move into a parsonage. I wanted to stay in my little home with my family and live a safe, happy life.

I was terrified of the future.

MOVING DAYS ARE FINALLY OVER

The last time I moved was almost twenty years ago, when I bought this home in the country. I've really lost track of the time, and the only thing that reminds me of how many years I've been here is my monthly mortgage payment. Since I am still paying it, I know that 30 years hasn't passed, because that's the length of the mortgage.

I remember that move from my little home to our first parsonage all too well, as I remember every move, until the one where I moved out of parsonages forever. Since then, the two moves I've made have been much less traumatic or memorable, and they have been on my own terms, not because of some committee's decision or the fears and insecurities of my preacher-husband.

With my last move from the parsonage, I loaded up most of my precious wedding gifts – those china plates, the crystal, and silver - that I'd lugged with me from place to place for 20 years. I now have kitchen cabinets with no doors on them, so I can see my treasures every time I go into my kitchen. I use my crystal on a regular basis for my wine, margaritas, mojitos and martinis. When I am in a festive mood, I'll have dinner on my Wedgwood china and use my sterling silver flatware. I left all of the silver-plate trays with Chad – he'd need them for all of those blasted parsonage open houses. I've not missed them at all. In reality, I've used these things more since I've been alone than we ever did as a parsonage family.

I've also learned that to bloom where I am planted has changed in meaning from those early years. For one thing, I don't feel confined to a pot with soil packed around my roots, as I did in my preacher's wife years. I may have lived in the same home for almost 20 years now, but I feel as free as I ever have in my life, with my nourishing roots spread out beneath me, giving me strength and stability.

There was so much that being a preacher's wife taught me. There were many hard lessons to learn, and for a long time I was very bitter over having to learn them. But today I can honestly look back at those years and all that I experienced and see the lessons in each obstacle I faced and each uncomfortable situation I found myself in.

There were many years that I was truly planted, but never bloomed. I felt much like those plastic flower arrangements you see in cemeteries – stuck into a weatherproof pot, pretty but not alive or growing. I just existed, living each day to get through it to the next, and spending a lot of time in the future, wishing for things that couldn't be, and yearning for things that were out of my reach.

In many ways Chad was a highly successful minister. But in other ways he was a failure, both to himself and to his calling. And because I was the one closest to him, I felt each success and failure, and internalized them all, somehow believing that the blame resided in me whenever he faltered.

I once told Chad that I felt like a weight tied around his neck, dragging him down, not realizing that the weight was around my own neck, as well as his. And because I clung to him so fiercely, our combined weight probably did make it harder for him to maneuver. As an old woman, I have the privilege of looking back with clearer sight and seeing where we both had our issues, some more serious than others.

Chad's life also included dynamics and secrets that I didn't know about or understand, and wouldn't – for many years.

I look back at that first move, and ache for the young mother who was me. I wish I could reach back in time to comfort her, give her some advice, and give her courage. I am glad that all she is now is a memory, and all of that is behind her. Little did she know as she was packing up the belongings in her little home and selling her treasured furniture, that she was at the brink of becoming a person she never expected, or dreamed, of being. She also had no way of predicting the loneliness she'd experience, the invisibility she'd feel, or of the hurt she would experience in the next twenty years.

I wish she'd known then that she'd end up being me. Maybe that would have given her hope.

She might have also done some things differently, making the story I am telling a different one.

THE FIRST CHURCH

Our U-Haul truck was bulging at the seams. Even without a lot of furniture, we had tons of stuff and dozens of boxes to take to our new home, mostly those treasured wedding gifts and our children's toys. Chad was amazed that we had so many boxes, and commented on more than one occasion that we should get rid of some of it before moving. I couldn't bear to part with a thing. But I didn't dare even suggest that we didn't need them, or Chad would have them out in the front yard in a yard sale or he'd be carting them off either to Goodwill or to the local dump. He had no concept of sentiment, and anything that made his life more complicated was deemed of little or no value in his eyes.

I had to fight to keep everything I wanted, including the boys' toys. If Chad saw that they didn't play with a particular toy on a daily basis, he'd assume that the toy wasn't worth keeping, and it would disappear from the house. As we packed the truck on moving day, I watched him like a hawk, making sure that each box made it onto the truck and on its way to the parsonage.

The church that was assigned to Chad was an old, frame church, located about forty miles from the theology school where he would obtain his Master's Degree in Divinity. Part of the deal was that he would serve the church as its full-time pastor for a meager salary for three years while he was also a full-time student. With this appointment, Chad actually had two full-time jobs. The other part of the deal was that the church would provide us with their furnished parsonage to live in. We were sternly reminded that this was not really our home, but the church's, and it was our responsibility to take care of it while we were there. We wouldn't have to pay rent, but I was worried about how we would make it financially.

Chad assured me that his tuition was taken care of. He received a scholarship from the church, and he took the profit we'd made on the sale of our house to cover the rest of his tuition.

"Don't worry about it, Fran," he assured me repeatedly. "Everything will work out. God will take care of us."

In my mind, I answered back, "God is taking care of you. What about me and our children?" I didn't dare cross my husband out loud.

I wanted to believe that God was there to watch over me, but I didn't have the faith that Chad had. I worried constantly about finances. I prayed for guidance and for strength, but felt like my prayers hit the ceiling only to bounce back at me. I wondered why God had called Chad into his ministry, but he never gave me any reassurance at all that I was part of the bargain. As I drove the car with the boys out of our driveway, following the moving truck with Chad driving, I thought I was going to throw up. I felt completely empty, and a dark cloud of apprehension hung over me. I tried to keep the boys from seeing my despair and fear, and kept them talking and singing silly children's songs as we followed the truck down the highway.

After the two-hour drive to our new church and home, we pulled into the gravel parking lot of the little church and followed it around back to the driveway to the parsonage. We were alone. Nobody was there to meet us, to welcome us to our new church home, or to even say "hello." In a way I was relieved, although I felt very odd walking up the steps to the house, trying the doorknob to find the door unlocked, and stepping into the kitchen of this house that was to be our home.

The kids were delighted. Before I could stop them, Dan had darted into the house, followed by toddling Kent, and both were busy exploring the rooms. Soon I heard Dan call out that they had found their room and were shouting that it had two "big boy beds" in it. When I took a look, I saw that it was small and crowded, and I knew that there was no way Kent's crib was going to fit in there. We later solved the problem by pushing one bed up against a wall and inserting a portable bed rail that we had used for Dan in his transition from baby bed to twin bed.

The excitement of my little sons was contagious, and I soon found myself shedding my apprehension and fear and picking up on their positive energy.

With this parsonage, I had my first experience of *Parsonage Green*. I learned that this was a common joke among the ministers' wives that I would meet over the next several years, as the common prominent color of almost every parsonage interior design I moved into was labeled *celery* on paint swatches. With this parsonage, the word "design" would be an overstatement, but whoever decorated it must have gotten the *Parsonage Green* memo. There was nothing wrong with the house. It was large enough for our family, was clean and neat, and in my eyes, sterile. There just wasn't anything about it that felt like home. I was very glad that I had insisted on bringing our personal possessions with me. The few lamps, pictures, and other knickknacks I insisted on keeping would make it feel more like it was my home, I was sure.

We had been unloading the truck for at least an hour, when a car pulled up into the drive and a middle-aged man and woman and two teen-age girls climbed out. The woman was carrying a casserole dish, and the girls each had a grocery bag, which they carried as they came up the house steps. The man went straight to the truck, shook Chad's hand and began helping unload it.

I watched as all of this unfolded, wondering what I'd say to this stranger who was entering my house. It surprised me that she didn't knock, but came right inside, heading for the kitchen. She knew where it was! It didn't occur to me that this was actually her house, as a church member, and that no doubt she had been here many times before. Being a preacher's wife was brand new to me, and this was my first afternoon of being the first lady of the parsonage.

There was much to learn.

A TRIP DOWN MEMORY LANE

I drove past that parsonage not long ago.

I had gone up to North Georgia to buy some fresh apples for making applesauce and jelly, and decided to detour out of curiosity and out of a little nostalgia. It took me quite awhile to find the place.

When we moved to our first church, it was a rural church on the outskirts of a small metropolitan town. The church had been nestled under large oak trees on a dirt road. It took me awhile and a few turn-arounds, but I finally found it.

A freeway now passes through the town, with circling access roads and confusing exits. All of the old landmarks were gone, replaced by a Marriott hotel and strip malls galore. Once I located the road leading to the church, time stood still, and I was passing familiar homes of former church members. Progress and growth hadn't yet tarnished this section of town. The narrow road leading to the church was now paved, and I made the right turn out of a long-forgotten habit. There it stood, the little white church and brick parsonage. I thought I could see my little boys swinging on the swing set in the yard.

Blinking myself back to the present, I took a closer look at things. Really, nothing seemed different, except for the name of the minister on the church sign. I pulled into the parking area and stopped the car. I didn't turn off the engine. I didn't get out. I didn't want to be seen.

The church appeared to be closed – no lights were on and no other cars were in the lot. The minister must be away at school. As I moved my focus to the parsonage, my eyes went past the modern version of my sons' swing set, not in use at the moment. A car sat in the driveway, and I could see a light on through the window, the one where I used to stand and gaze out of, wondering what on earth was I doing there.

I remembered an autumn day when Dan, Kent and I were standing at the window watching the leaves fall. Chad was at the church officiating at a wedding, and we'd been instructed to stay indoors until after the wedding was over and the guests were gone.

As we stood at that window, Danny looked up at me and asked me, "Where's Daddy?"

"He's right over there, at the church, marrying somebody," was my offhand response.

Dan burst into tears. I asked him what was wrong, and he sobbed, "He can't do that to us, Mommy. He's married to you!"

It took me quite awhile to console him and assure him that his daddy wasn't leaving us to marry someone else, but that he was helping a young couple get married to each other.

As I gazed at the parsonage from a distance of his lifetime and mine, I saw that the fear of abandonment was very real for Dan, and he sensed, if not knew, that his little life wasn't on firm ground. Mine wasn't either, and I ached for my small son. But I was stuck there, just as my sons were, and I was determined to make the best of it - whatever *it* was.

So, here I was, sitting in my idling car, reminiscing and remembering. The one thing that strikes me now about this day was the knowledge that all I had to do was put my car into *Drive*, hit the accelerator, and I could leave.

Back in those early days, this was not an option for me.

BECOMING A MINISTER'S WIFE

My education began in earnest that first day with strangers in my new home, putting groceries into the cupboards, the casserole into the oven, setting my table with paper goods they had brought with them, and generally making themselves at home.

The family who greeted us on moving day, Jim and Sheila, along with their teen-age daughters, Meg and Holly, soon became the closest things we would have to friends for the three years we were at Pleasant Hill Southern Evangelical Church. Long-time Evangelicals, they had seen "parsonage families" as we were now labeled, come and go, and had stories to tell about them all. I mused as we sat at the dining room table together to eat Sheila's Chicken-Bean Casserole, what stories about us they'd be telling the next parsonage family three years from now.

I appreciated their help, really I did. But I felt like it was an invasion at the time. They knew my new home better than I did, and had their own ideas about where things should go, and who should sleep in which room. I watched as Sheila hung my clothes in the closet she dubbed the Master Bedroom. I would have preferred for the boys to share this room, since it was the largest and the closest to the one bathroom in the house, but I didn't have a say in the matter. This room had a double bed in it, and the other two had twin beds. I never thought about switching beds from one room to the other. I was too new to this new life to venture expressing my own opinion.

Dan and Kent headed to the back of the house to their room, pulling Meg and Holly by their little hands to make beds and unpack toys. They couldn't wait to play with their new friends.

Sheila and I chatted as I accepted her help in unpacking my kitchen things. It was all so odd to me. As I opened the kitchen cabinets, I saw that all of the shelves were freshly lined with plastic liner that had pumpkins and other orange and green vegetables printed on it. These were the days of *Harvest Gold* and *Avocado Green*, so the shelf liner complimented the green appliances in the kitchen and the Parsonage Green walls. I hated it already.

I liked Sheila from the start, but I wasn't sure if a friendship was in the cards for us. I'd been warned by Joan about getting too close to parishioners, and to "never, ever in a million years confide in someone in the church. You'd be amazed at the versions of what you really said that you'll hear coming back at you." Always one to take advice to heart, whether it was good or not, I instinctively knew that this probably was a pretty good piece to follow. I sometimes slipped and didn't follow her advice, and sure enough, it always came back to bite me.

Meg and Holly took to my little boys immediately, and the feeling was mutual. When they offered their babysitting services, I knew that my children would be in good hands with them. My only problem was that I had no money, and knew that I'd never be able to afford to pay them to watch the boys. Chad kept telling me not to worry about money, and he gave me a certain amount each month allotted by category to buy groceries, gasoline, and anything else either the boys or I needed. It seemed I always ran out of money before I ran out of month, so of course I worried despite what he said.

Sheila and Jim, and the girls, stayed at the house until the truck was unloaded and everything was inside the house. Most of the boxes had been unpacked, thanks to Sheila's seemingly boundless energy, and we were ready to spend our first night in the parsonage. I wasn't happy, but I didn't know exactly how I felt. I didn't want the boys to sense my feelings, so I put on my happy mask, one that became a part of me over the next several years. Nobody would ever see how I really felt, if I could help it. My husband had been called by God to enter the ministry, and I was not going to argue with God or question his will, a promise I'd make over and over and would break just as many times.

Chad was very excited about this new adventure, and as soon as he told the boys goodnight and helped me tuck them into their new beds, he headed across the parking lot to the little church office to begin working on his first sermon, leaving me alone in the *Parsonage Green* house with all of my fears and insecurities swarming around me.

Moving day was on a Thursday, so I had two days to prepare myself for my first Sunday as Preacher's Wife. Most of the time was spent rearranging my kitchen cabinets and putting things where I wanted them, not where Sheila did. Dan and Kent settled into their new home quickly, and soon their room looked just like their bedroom in their previous home – cluttered with toys. I took down the purple floral curtains that hung at the two windows in their room, replacing them with the Noah's Ark ones that I had made when Kent was born. Luckily, they fit the windows, and added a home touch that I desperately needed for my little boys' room. Kent had still been in a crib before we moved, but now he was in his "big boy" bed, the twin bed with portable rail. He loved it, and didn't miss his crib at all.

It was quiet. Nobody came to visit us or meet us, and I began to wonder if the church members knew we had moved in. My insecurities grew, and I couldn't shake the anxiety. Chad was in over-drive. When he wasn't at the church rummaging around or working in his tiny office, he was pacing the house looking for something to do, which only added to my nervousness.

On Saturday afternoon, I talked him into taking the boys to a nearby park, where they played on the playground equipment while we sat on a bench and watched them, and then we splurged and ate at a local taco place. We didn't talk much during those first days. I didn't know what to say, and being on the verge of tears all the time, I didn't want to get something started between us. I couldn't let Chad know that I was filled with anxiety. He wouldn't understand, and I knew all I'd get back from him was, "Don't worry. God will take care of us."

Sunday morning arrived before I was ready for it. I got the boys up, fed, and dressed, and then began to work on myself. Chad had gotten up early, fixed a bowl of cereal, and bee-lined for the church. I selected a modest summer dress that I had made, put on a little make-up (not too much, of course), checked myself out in the mirror, and decided that I looked presentable.

When it was time for Sunday School to begin, I rounded up the boys, and together we made our first trip across the parking lot to church.

ANY QUESTIONS?

I don't attend Sunday School. I only go to church sporadically.

When I think about that first Sunday, and all of the first Sundays as a preacher's wife, I get a sinking, sick feeling in the pit of my stomach, remembering. I was not cut out to be in the spotlight, and nothing about the parsonage life came natural to me. I look back at myself, and it's as though I am gazing at another person, while reliving the same emotions and feelings.

There were many first Sundays during my marriage to Chad, and they never got easier. I remember the huge relief at the end of our marriage, after the split had been made, when I realized that I never had to set foot in another church if I didn't want to.

In many ways I am still the same person that I was so many years ago. I shun situations where I don't know people, and am uncomfortable in crowded, social functions. I know who I am, which I didn't back then. In those early days, I was stretched every which-way. Danny had a favorite toy when we moved to Pleasant

Hill called *Stretch Armstrong.* You could pull on the arms and legs of Stretch, and he'd grow to the length of a small room. When you let go of him, he'd return to his original shape. Sometimes I felt much like Stretch.

My silent fight with God began in earnest at that time as well. I was convinced that Chad was called by God to be a minister, but I didn't feel like I had received a call to be a minister's wife. I knew better than to argue with my creator, though, and out of fear and guilt, I kept quiet. It took me a long, long time to make my peace with God.

Today, looking back, I can question God and his calling, and I can even have misgivings about his call to Chad. As insecure as I was, Chad was even more so, but he could disguise it well with his outgoing personality and need to be accepted and respected.

Ministry was perfect for him. I sometimes play with the thought that ministry was not a calling, but an escape mechanism for him, and a kind of per-formance. He could hide behind the pulpit every Sunday, like a character in a play, standing in the spotlight of his adoring congregation, who hung on every word he uttered - boosting his self-esteem on a weekly basis. Chad became the character that God called into the ministry and played the part, thus releasing him from facing who he really was.

The ministry also relieved Chad of responsibility. The Southern Evangelical Church guaranteed him a church and home, as well as a pension. As long as he didn't get into ethical or moral troubles, he was set for life. The church also served as an escape valve for him. If things got uncomfortable for him, all he had to do was ask to be reassigned, and off we'd go to another church in another town. It didn't matter that his salary in those early years was a pittance, and that I constantly worried about our financial well-being; Chad seemed to worry about nothing.

My sons are grown now, and I am a senior citizen. Nothing in my home is *Parsonage Green*. Although I am retired, I continue to earn a small living from part-time work here and there and from selling my jellies. The parsonage years are a distant memory.

For the most part, Dan and Kent came through their growing up as preacher's kids with few permanent scars. We don't talk about religion or church much when we get together. I suspect that deep down they have some sort of faith, but outwardly they shun the church and everything it represents, whether true or false. But they are good kids, caring and loving, and treat others with compassion and generosity.

Somewhere something good rubbed off on them.

THE FIRST OF MANY FIRSTS

Somehow I made it through that first Sunday, finding myself once again in an adult Sunday School class. I made some enemies very quickly. I shunned the couples' class, and opted to attend the class for little old ladies. I found them to be honest and welcoming. I remember that Sunday School class with very warm memories. The six ladies in the class took me under their nurturing wings, and while they didn't become my friends, I felt very secure in their class. They never pressured me to join in on the discussions, and while I had to pray out loud at times, I didn't feel like I was being judged for what I had to say to God. I was still very young, and they offered a huge amount of wisdom, which I absorbed with gratitude.

What I didn't see was the wall that I unintentionally built between myself and the members of the couples' class. They felt as though I had snubbed them. What made matters worse was that Chad gravitated to this group, and often taught their class. He was one-half of a couple, and they didn't like it that his other half was sitting in the next classroom with their mothers. In the three years that we were at Pleasant Hill, I never felt as if they particularly liked me. They were smitten with Chad, however, and never hesitated to tell me after a church service how much they loved him. It seemed to me that they enjoyed rubbing salt into my fresh preacher's wife wounds.

I also discovered the sanctity of church pews. I made the mistake that first Sunday of choosing a pew that had been claimed a generation back by a founding church family. I had settled down into the pew with Danny and Kent, when a kind-sounding elderly woman approached us and gently told us that we'd have to move – this was her family's pew. We quickly picked up our things, and resettled ourselves one row behind. Thankfully, this pew wasn't claimed, and we didn't have to get up and move again. I made a mental note that this pew was safe for my boys and me. We sat through our first worship service, and I was actually impressed with Chad's sermon. Being the first one he had ever delivered, I was on pins and needles over what he was going to say or how he would be accepted.

Like I said, Chad's sermon was pretty good. He took the opportunity to share with his new congregation his calling into ministry. It was interesting to me listening to it, because in all of our married life, he never told me much about how he felt, only what we were going to do. In his message, he spoke about trying to deny the call and attempting to ignore it. In my opinion, he left out a lot of information that I thought was important in explaining how we arrived at this point, but again I conceded to God's plan, and felt inspired to do the best job I could as his wife and head helpmate – whatever that meant.

The church service was followed by a covered dish dinner to welcome the new parsonage family. I was very happy to have my two little boys with me, because I could concentrate on them and make sure that they behaved and ate a good lunch. I didn't have to talk very much to anyone, instead hiding behind my children and letting them be the social butterflies that I wasn't able to be. Chad wasn't around to help me fill their plates or find them a place to eat, but thankfully Meg and Holly appeared at my side in the buffet line to help me with the boys. I was most grateful for these two wonderful teen-age girls.

Late in the afternoon we were relaxing in our living room watching television when we heard a knock on our back door. I couldn't imagine who it might be, since we didn't know anybody yet. Chad got up and went to the door. I heard a loud commotion, and before I could get up and out of my chair, in piled dozens of people, all church members, led by Jim and Sheila, carrying grocery bags and shouting "You've been pounded!"

I was at a loss - I had no idea what was going on - but I certainly didn't like all of these unwelcome visitors intruding on my personal space. However, I was soon overwhelmed with the generosity of these strangers. Unpacked and unloaded onto the kitchen counter and dining room table were groceries – pounds of them. We were given pounds of ground beef, bacon, flour, sugar, canned vegetables, eggs, cheese, shortening, cereals – everything you could imagine that we might need. Again, I met the same folks who had been in church earlier in the day, but they seemed to be much more relaxed and friendly, and appeared to thoroughly enjoy the success of their surprise.

And, best of all, they didn't stay long. After unpacking all of the grocery bags, they milled around the parsonage for a little while, and then they were gone, just as quickly as they had arrived. I had never heard of pounding parties; this seemed to be a southern country tradition, and as the years passed, I encountered them with almost every move we made. It wasn't until Chad moved up in the system to the more suburban churches that our poundings stopped, and welcoming parties took on a more sophisticated air.

I had been a church-attender all my life, but I was now experiencing the church from a new view, and one that I already had conflicting thoughts about. On one hand, I was astounded by the pounding, while on the other hand I was already feeling the invisible wall that separated me from the people in the church.

This Sunday was the first of a series of first Sundays over Chad's career. I dreaded every one, and they never got easier. Each church we served had its own unique customs for welcoming the new preacher and his family, all very unnerving for me and filling me with fear and insecurity.

In fact, looking back, this one was probably the easiest of them all!

ONE PREACHER'S WIFE TO ANOTHER

I am meeting my minister's wife, Kelly, for lunch at a little restaurant in town this week. I made a point to get to know her when she and her husband moved to the Wellspring church.

Kelly is about fifteen years younger than I am, and older than I was when I shut the last parsonage door behind me. We have very little in common, except for the preacher's wife bond, which is enough to bind the most different of people together. Kelly married her husband later in life than I did, and she already had a career of her own. She also knew who she was marrying and what she was getting into, as much as anyone can foresee the future. Unlike the young me, she is very much her own person, and has an identity apart from her husband, the preacher. We get to-gether for lunch on occasion when she is off from work, or on a holiday.

I'll never forget the first lunch we had together. She was a bit curious about why I'd invite her out, since we didn't know each other very well, and I don't participate in church activities. When we met at the restaurant that first time, it was a little awkward and stilted, so I filled her in right off the bat the motive behind my madness. After telling her, "I was also married to a minister", and after the blank stare of disbelief as she absorbed this bit of news, she leaned back in her chair, and asked, "When?" I guess she had so many questions, the first thing in order was to find out the time frame for this admission.

"It's been awhile," I offered. "We were married for 25 years – 20 of them were in the ministry. We divorced 20 years ago."

Kelly's entire body relaxed, and she let out a sigh. "Is this why you invited me today?" she asked.

I admitted that it was.

More questions followed, which I answered as honestly as I could. Some of my history is mine alone, and I didn't share it with her, but she got the jist of the story. As we left the restaurant, she asked me if we could do it again soon. Since that day, we've managed to get together about once a month. During our lunch times together, I've learned more about the members of our little church than I ever wanted to know.

I guess I feel a little bit cocky over my friendship with Kelly. She confides in me, and lets her hair down with me. I listen to her talk about the parsonage and parsonage committee, and listen to her complaints about the house, about its location on the church property, and about how she feels like there is a revolving door into her kitchen where people come and go, invited or not. She even has to deal with *Parsonage Green*. The first time I visited her at the parsonage, I was shocked to see the living room – I would have thought that a few decades would have changed the mindset of parsonage decorating committees.

I nod my head and say to her, "I know exactly what you're talking about."

Inside I am thinking, "I'm so glad it's you and not me, honey. I don't have to put up with any of that anymore."

But I am glad that she has me and that I have her for a friend. I feel like I have something to offer her in an understanding and listening ear, and she knows that she can say anything she feels like to me, and doesn't have to worry about it coming back to bite her.

I am no longer a preacher's wife, but I will always be a preacher's wife. I can't erase all of those years. I wouldn't want to. Even though it was a huge misfit for me, there were many good times, and through my journeys from one parsonage to another and from one church to the next, I collected a huge scrapbook of memories, and learned life lessons I might have missed otherwise.

Kelly reminds me of my past, helps me celebrate my present, and hopefully looks toward the future with me. I'm very glad that we are friends.

THE FIRST CHURCH, THEOLOGY SCHOOL, LESSONS LEARNED

My education of living in the fishbowl named The Parsonage began in earnest during the three years we were at Pleasant Hill. I learned lots of lessons, got burned quite a few times, licked my wounds, and kept on, mostly under the sincere belief that this was God's calling and will for my life and Chad's. My parents were my chief cheerleaders, and whenever I became disenchanted, they were there to remind me of my responsibility to support Chad, be a good minister's wife, and suck it up.

They weren't bad years, but they weren't what I envisioned in my naïve imagination. Being a minister's wife presented challenges I never would have dreamed about, much less yearned for. However, in spite of the loneliness, the barbs thrown in my direction, and the shock of really living in a fishbowl, the three years passed quickly, and somehow I maneuvered my way through them.

I learned the first week that we were at Pleasant Hill that I was in charge of the church bulletin. What a surprise this was for me, as I had never taken typing classes in school. I was strictly a hunt-and-peck typist, and not a good one at that. I also didn't know a thing about mimeograph machines, the forerunner of the clean and easy digital copier.

We had a room in the parsonage that served a dual purpose - laundry room, playroom, and typing room. Furnished along with the washer and dryer was an old manual typewriter. Chad showed me how to type onto the film that would be put onto the roller of the mimeograph machine, and how to correct mistakes using a bottle of foul smelling liquid with its little brush to cover up the incorrect letters and numbers. It didn't take me long to realize that smelling that stuff gave me severe headaches, and I made so many mistakes, I always ended up with a doozy of one.

Chad gave me his sermon title, selected hymns, and announcements on Wednesday, and I had to have the bulletin ready for the mimeograph machine by Saturday afternoon, when we'd go over to the church together, run off the bulletins and fold them. After my first attempt at the blasted machine when I got purple ink all over myself, my shirt, and the work table, Chad decided that it was too complicated for me to run, and he took on the task of printing the bulletins. Most weeks I put off typing the bulletin until the last minute, because I hated it so.

I complained to Chad that I thought this was something a church member should do, but he didn't listen to me. Almost every Sunday someone would find an error in the bulletin, which embarrassed me greatly, but Chad would only laugh and make a comment about my poor typing skills. He was a terrible speller, so he seldom noticed my mistakes, but he seemed to enjoy it whenever someone else did. If anyone ever volunteered to take the job, Chad never told me. For three years this was my assigned task, and I actually improved my typing ability and gained some confidence in the process.

The piano also came into play during the first couple of months we were there. Miss Ida was the church pianist, and she took her job very seriously. Her skills at the piano left a lot to be desired - for many hymns she played only the melody with one hand - and if it weren't for our terrific organist, Sunday morning singing would have been a disaster. Tom, the organist, pumped up the volume on the organ so that Miss Ida's mistakes weren't quite so noticeable.

At one of the early Administrative Board meetings, at which I wasn't invited to attend, Miss Ida announced that she was going to be away the month of August, and wouldn't be available to play the piano during the morning services. Chad, thinking of me and my need to get involved and be included in the church activities, shared with the council that I could play the piano. It seemed the perfect solution – I'd fill in for Miss Ida. Without asking me if I'd like to take on this job, Chad volunteered my services. I was a pretty good pianist, and grew up playing hymns, but I had never played in public before, except for yearly piano class recitals at which I usually froze up and messed up royally. The week before my debut performance, I was at the church every afternoon going over the hymns and responses. Tom assured me that I didn't need to worry about the prelude or postlude - that this was strictly for the organ. While I went over the hymns, Dan and Kent played in the church nursery, or raced around the sanctuary, climbing on the altar railing or crawling in and out of the pews.

By Sunday, I was ready, but shaking in my shoes from an extreme case of stage fright. My biggest mistake that day was in doing very well. I played the hymns flawlessly and kept up with Tom's organ playing to a tee. The outcome was better than I'd expected, and after the service, people swarmed in my direction complimenting me. I continued with this schedule of practicing and accompanying for the next three Sundays, and was quite relieved to know that Miss Ida would be returning to her post.

What I didn't know was that the church chatter was in high gear over the phone lines as church members began hatching a scheme to get Miss Ida off of the piano bench permanently. Tom was the one who alerted me to the gossip mill, and asked me what I intended to do. Since I knew nothing about this, I told him I had no intention of becoming the church pianist. I did not want the job.

I spoke to Chad about the problem, and he assured me that he would handle it. If that had been all there was to solving the problem, it wouldn't have been so bad, but somehow the gossip reached Miss Ida's ears upon her return from vacation, and she was livid. She had been the pianist for forty years, and no little preacher's wife was going to unseat her! She lashed out at Chad about it.

Chad, being a diplomat at heart, wanted to ease her anger, but he also had heard an earful from church members about her terrible piano playing, so he was caught in the middle. He attempted to calm Miss Ida's hurt feelings, but deep inside I think he wanted me to take her job. He felt like it might help the worship services and bring in more members if the Sunday music wasn't such a disaster each week.

Well, Miss Ida assumed that I was the instigator of the piano coup, and even though she was rightfully re-seated at her place the next Sunday, she never liked me, and was always cool toward me. I decided to stay away from the church piano from that point on, and if I had the need to make some music, I would do so in private when nobody was in the church. Tom was very disappointed in the outcome, but he took it like the wonderful musician and gentleman that he was, and kept the organ at full volume.

Another lesson I learned early on was to make sure I didn't duplicate a covered dish for any of the church's dinners. It was a small church, barely 100 members in all, and most of the members had been there since infant baptism. Each family had its specialty that was proudly prepared and lovingly brought to the monthly fellowship suppers. I wasn't aware of this when I prepared a broccoli-cheese casserole for the first dinner we attended. The Fisher family was in charge of broccoli-cheese casserole, and Kitty Fisher was the master of the casserole. When I placed my dish on the table next to hers, one of the other members looked at me and asked, "Didn't you know that this dish was already covered?"

I took her question literally, with it being a covered dish dinner, and answered, "I didn't think it needed to be covered, since we'll be eating so soon."

That one innocent statement saved the day for me. She laughed, took me aside, and explained the protocol. Thankfully, Kitty's casserole was much better than mine, so in the long run, this didn't cause a huge church crisis, and I got off the hook pretty easily.

The next week, I called Sheila on the phone and asked her if she could write down a list of whose specialty was what, so that I wouldn't make this mistake again. If it happened again, the consequences might not be as minor. I became the pizza maker for covered dish dinners, which nobody else in the church made. The kids loved it, so I was from that time on a hit with them. Pizza became my trademark specialty for many years and for many church dinners.

September arrived, and Chad began his studies to become a real minister. He loved being in school, and we seldom saw him, except on weekends and holidays. We settled into his schedule of ministry and student.

There were no theology classes on Mondays, because so many of the students were also serving churches.

Chad used Mondays to begin his sermon preparation and make church visits. We didn't see much of him on Mondays. The other four days of the week, he'd leave before dawn, come home in time for dinner, and then disappear in his little study until after the boys and I had gone to bed.

The days were very long for me. Our parsonage, set as it was at the edge of the church property, was very isolated. We had no neighbors, and the boys weren't yet old enough for school. Thank goodness, Dan and Kent were close. They played very well together and didn't seem to mind not having other children to play with. A lot of the time I was bored, and longed to be in school myself, have a job - anything that would make the long days pass faster. I spent my days taking care of the house, playing with the boys, watching Sesame Street and other children's television programs, and reading.

I was thankful that I had a car, and wasn't stuck in the parsonage without wheels. Grocery shopping became an event for the boys and me, and we looked forward to our weekly trip to the store. I lived for the weekends when Chad would be home and we might do something fun. We had no spare money, but we often went on picnics or hikes at a nearby state park. I even began to look forward to Sundays, because at least I would have the opportunity to talk to other adults.

Even though I had a car, I felt trapped. When we moved to Pleasant Hill, Chad put us on an even stricter budget than when he was teaching. As always, he handled all of the finances. I didn't even have access to a checkbook or know what we had in the bank. Each month, when Chad received his paycheck, he would bring cash home and put it into a folder he had made that had pockets for each of my areas of expenditures: groceries, children's clothes, gasoline, entertainment, my miscellaneous needs. I had to make do with what he allotted. If I spent too much in one category, then another would suffer until the next month. He took care of all of the major expenses. Chad had determined that I only needed to buy one tankful of gasoline for my car each month, so I really had to watch where we went during the days so that I wouldn't run out before the month was over.

I was never aware of him putting himself on a strict budget. He always seemed to have cash for things he needed or wanted. I didn't question him, though, because I had faith that he was being a good steward of our money.

Chad was very concerned over how I looked and dressed, and wanted me to always look like what he thought a preacher's wife should look like. This was a challenge on our tight budget, even though I made most of my own clothes. Not only did I save money doing this, but it took up some of my time, and I enjoyed the creativity of making something that wasn't straight off of a department store rack.

At home, however, he complained about my choice of clothes. He didn't like for me to wear blue jeans and sweat shirts, or shorts in the summer, even around the house. He didn't feel like this was appropriate dress. I objected to this, and won on principle, although I promised him that I would always dress nicely whenever I went somewhere, or if something was going on over at the church while I was at home.

What I didn't know at the time was that the preacher's wife who preceded me was "a slob," as Sheila confided to me one day. The Pastor-Parish Committee had told Chad about her at his first meeting with them, and he took it on himself to make sure I didn't join her in this category. Now that he was a minister, it became even more important to him than ever that I look good, which in turn made him look good.

It was also during these early days that I began to lose myself in the mirror and to feel invisible. Chad was clearly the star in our family. He took center stage every Sunday morning, and as time passed, his sermons got better and better. He had a wonderful comedic sense of timing, and could have the congregation laughing while challenging them in their Christian life. I had little identity – I was his wife and Dan and Kent's mommy. I did what he volunteered me to do in the church, and I kept my distance when I wasn't invited to participate.

At first, when a church member would greet me after church to say, "We just love Chad. His sermon was wonderful today," I'd beam with pride and say a modest "Thank you."

Later, I began muttering under my breath where no one could hear, "Why don't you just tell him that? I don't need to hear your praises of him."

I was crying out inside, "What about me? Doesn't anybody know that I am here?" It was childish and self-centered on my part, but there was very little in my life to confirm that I was doing anything worthwhile.

PARSONAGE OPEN HOUSES

Every year at Christmas time, I invite all of my family, relatives and friends to my home for a Saturday of Christmas cookie baking. We begin early in the morning, and bake cookies all day long, finishing when the countertops are overflowing with cookies of all sorts and everyone is getting sick from eating cookie dough and sampling new kinds of cookies. We order out pizza for lunch, and snack our way through the day eating, drinking, decorating, cooking, and making a terrific mess in my kitchen.

Everyone brings a big box to fill up with cookies to take home, and empty the counters much quicker than we loaded them up. My entire home is open to my guests, and when the day is over, I often find cookie crumbs and empty drink cups in my bathroom, my closet, and my bedroom. There isn't an inch in my home that is off-limits to all the children who come to my annual event.

I do a little decorating in preparation, but beyond that, my house only gets a lick and a promise of cleaning and straightening. Everyone knows that Aunt Fran's house is an adventure in itself, and there's not much in it that is sacred or untouchable. This day each year is the highlight of my Christmas season, and after Cookie Baking Day is over, I feel like I have celebrated my Christmas.

This is my choice of how I like to usher in the holidays. It is very different from the traditional Parsonage Open House, that I endured hosting every year I lived in a parsonage.

My first Open House was the first year I was a Parsonage Wife. The Pastor-Parish Committee, along with the Parsonage Committee, informed Chad that our open house would be the Sunday before Christmas. He, in turn, filled me in on this bit of news. Again, I turned to Sheila, who gave me the nitty-gritty of what was in store for me.

On Open House day, she told me, the parsonage would be open for all members to come over for refreshments that I'd prepare for them. While at the house, they would have the opportunity to walk through it to see how their parsonage family was living, and to make sure that we were taking care of it. I had never experienced a white glove inspection, but Sheila's description of the day made me think that Parsonage Open House was such an event.

It was our responsibility to have the house decorated for Christmas and to be dressed in our holiday festive best. The open house would last from 2:00 pm until 6:00 pm, when visitors could come and go. Sheila assured me that there would probably be twenty people or less in the house at any given time. She also volunteered Meg and Holly to serve punch and make sure there was plenty of food on the table, and she volunteered herself to be stationed in the kitchen to assist with dishwashing, filling trays, and anything else that might need to be done. She didn't volunteer to help me clean the house in preparation for the big day, which I certainly would have taken her up on.

I spent the entire week prior to Open House Day cleaning, dusting, polishing, cooking, organizing, and worrying. I made every kind of cookie that I had recipes for, and my mother sent me a homemade fruitcake to serve. I spent almost my entire cash allotment for the month on punch mix, Christmas napkins, plates and cups, and ingredients for everything I was baking. Chad helped by staying out of my way, although he and the boys took on the job of getting the Christmas tree, setting it up, and decorating it.

By the time Sunday arrived, I was exhausted. The house was neat and orderly - pretty sterile looking in my opinion, and I had bribed the boys not to pull out any toys that morning.

As soon as we got home from church, I did a whirlwind last-minute trip through the house, made sure all the closet doors were shut, and the toilet in our one bathroom was clean. I had to admit that the house looked very nice. A Christmas tablecloth added a nice touch to the dining room, and the Christmas tree with all its lights and ornaments was festive. You could tell that it had been decorated by two little boys, but I thought it looked wonderful.

Promptly at 2:00 pm, Sheila, Jim, Meg, and Holly appeared. Jim took over Chad, and the ladies took over the kitchen and dining room. It wasn't long after that the first guests arrived, and Parsonage Open House began. It amazed me how people came in, helped themselves to the food, and proceeded to walk through the house. They even opened our closet doors to see what was in them! One well-meaning lady made a suggestion to me of how I should rearrange the furniture in the boys' bedroom. It was a full-scale invasion, complete with Christmas music, punch, and cookies. I hated it, but I smiled, chatted, and played the gracious hostess. Chad loved it. He was the hit of the day, joking, telling stories, and kidding around with the children. He was definitely in his element, while I was dying inside.

When 6:00 came and the final guest headed out the door, I collapsed onto the sofa in a heap. Chad came and sat next to me and handed an envelope to me. The chairman of the Pastor-Parish Committee had slipped it to him during the party, and he hadn't had a chance to look at it. Opening it, I saw bills, four of them. Hundred dollar bills. The note said that a love offering had been taken among the church members, and they all wished us a *Very Merry Christmas*. I was flabbergasted. I had never seen that much cash at one time in my life. Chad asked me what we should do with it. First, I offered, we should use some of it to pay for groceries for the rest of the month. He frowned at me, but begrudgingly agreed. Together we decided that some of it would help finance Santa Claus for the boys, and what was left over should go into a vacation fund. It almost made it worth it to have the Parsonage Open House.

Almost, but not quite.

So it was that I survived my first Parsonage Open House. I highly prefer my Cookie Baking Day!

THEOLOGY SCHOOL, PREACHING, AND SEX

Even though Chad was running on over-drive with theology school, pastoring the church complete with weddings, funerals, hospital and home visitations, he was still very demanding on an intimate basis. It seemed to take on a frantic nature to me, however, as we hardly ever had any time for just the two of us.

Sex became either a late-night, middle-of-the-night, or pre-dawn activity, and it seldom lasted longer than a few minutes. Romance or foreplay was not an option – that hadn't changed - and I wasn't ever consulted on what I wanted or when I wanted it. Many nights, Chad woke me up in the middle of the night telling me he couldn't sleep and needed to have sex. After the act, he'd be snoring away on his side of the bed, and I'd be wide awake, asking myself what had just happened. I voiced my feeling one time to him that I "feel like all I am is a hole." To which he took great offense, got angry with me for saying it, but did nothing to change anything. He seemed to me to be consumed with needing to have orgasms, and I was simply a convenient means to an end. Middle of the night was almost the only time we could have intimate moments without worrying about being interrupted, since it sometimes felt like our house had an open door policy for the church members to drop by at any time.

All of my lacy negligees from my hope chest were packed back in the chest, and I opted for oversized t-shirts or flannel gowns for my bedroom attire. I felt anything but sexy in those days, accepting the changes as something that was part of a normal marriage. I believed that as long as our lovemaking was frequent - which it certainly was - everything was OK.

One of my high school girlfriends once asked me if we had good sex. Looking at my marriage, I immediately answered "yes", but then when I thought about it really hard, it sunk in that a lot of sex didn't necessarily equal good sex. I began to consider that I might be missing something.

I could tell that some of the young single women in the church had crushes on Chad. They swooned all over him after church services, and made sure that they sat near him at church dinners. His personality carried him far, and he effortlessly wrapped the ladies around his little finger.

One in particular, Libby, went to all extremes to be near him. She was in her early twenties (a few years younger than me), single, and about fifty pounds overweight. She volunteered for everything that she thought Chad would be involved in. She even invited us over to her apartment for dinner one night, and spent the entire evening waiting hand and foot on him, and practically ignoring the fact that I or the boys were in the same room.

I was amused by it all – I knew from the way Chad always wanted me to look good and stay attractive and fit, that there was no way he'd be beguiled by her. He soaked it all in, thought she was a great Christian to do so much work in the church, and seemed to enjoy all her pawing. I remember our last Sunday at Pleasant Hill, when everyone was wishing us well with our next appointment, she sobbed and sobbed, and was not able to contain herself with any resemblance of decorum.

Chad loved the women in the church. In fact, he got along with them much better than with the men. He could get his way with anything he wanted to do by simply going to a Southern Evangelical's Women's meeting to state his case and present his latest great idea.

I didn't think anything strange about this – this was how he won my heart. I watched from a distance, a little jealous that he found it so easy to mingle and chat with them, while I felt like an outsider who couldn't break into the in-crowd. He became an honorary member of every women's group in the church.

With the men, he seemed to always be on edge, and constantly seeking their approval. I cringed at the way he would interact with them. It looked to me like he was always trying just a little too hard to fit in and to be liked, and often I would be embarrassed at some of the things he'd do or the way he would act while with a group of men. He was more like a little boy looking for attention through acting silly than a grown man and minister of a church. I didn't understand him at all, but again I didn't question. I simply observed, prayed, and tried to see everything as God's will.

Our first year passed, quickly at times, and as slow as a snail's pace at others. I settled in to the routine of being a minister's wife, and put all of my attention on my two small sons. Then, the second year, another Parsonage Open House, and it, too, was gone.

Before I knew it, Chad was in his third and final year of theology school, and he began thinking about his next appointment. He had done decently in school, if not stellar. Chad wasn't much of a student. He stood solidly in the lower middle of his class scholastically. His strengths were in preaching, and he was promised a good appointment after graduation. Pleasant Hill had grown in membership during our first two years, and there was briefly talk about the church moving from a student appointment to one that could support a full-time minister. This idea was nixed by the church higher-ups. I wouldn't have minded staying there. Dan was going into first grade the next year, and I could put Kent into a pre-school and possibly find a part-time job for myself. I thought I would really like to get out of the house doing something worthwhile, and earning a little money of my own.

I also yearned to go back to school. I wanted to finish college, get a degree, and make my father proud of me. While Pleasant Hill was a small church, its location was very favorable, in my opinion. There was a state university not far away, and a business park only a few miles from us where companies were always advertising for office help in the local newspaper. I wanted to get back out into the world. I wanted to make friends and be with people who didn't care that my husband was a preacher, or even who didn't even know him at all.

Chad was getting itchy feet. He said he was getting bored with Pleasant Hill and wanted a change. While still wildly popular with the women, he had crossed a few of the male leaders of the church, and even though they said they wanted him to stay on as their pastor, he was more and more uncomfortable and ready to bail out, regardless of whether the church's status changed, or not. He had a deep fear of failure, and felt that his luck was running out with this particular congregation. He was eager to move on.

I had broached the subject with him of my either getting a part-time job or going back to school. He wasn't enthusiastic about either idea. His wagon was hitched to a Southern Evangelical star out there somewhere, and all he thought about was moving. He needed me to stay at home so that I could fully support him and be a good minister's wife.

"Your place is right here next to me" became a mantra I heard all of the time. It played a dual role – it made me feel needed, and it made me feel trapped.

I began to contemplate on what or who I needed, and I came to the realization that I might not need Chad to complete me as he seemed to need me.

I kept this to myself.

WHO AM I, ANYHOW?

I discovered through the years of being married to Chad that my identity was wrapped up in his. Even after I finally took the big step and returned to college to get my degree, I couldn't shake the attachment.

As soon as anyone, especially women, learned that I was married to a minister, the friendship relationship changed, as well as conversations, when I was around. This carried into the workplace whenever I stood up to him and took a job, even if it was only for a short period of time. Break room conversations took on different tones the minute I would walk in on somebody's joke or tale about their husbands, girlfriends, or whoever happened to be the topic of the conversation at the time.

Chad was my best friend and my only friend. As I write this account of my life, I realize that for a long time I didn't have a voice of my own. Truth is, I didn't talk much, except to my children and to Chad. And of course, to God - which were mostly questions - I didn't really expect an answer from him.

Chad and I talked a lot; rather, he talked and I listened. Most of the time when I'd bring up something that I felt was important to me, he'd say, "Fran, I know what you're going to say," or "I know how you feel." That pretty much sealed the deal on whatever conversation I wanted to have.

For Chad, on the other hand, I was a close and convenient sounding board. He bared his soul to me about his discontent with a particular church or set of circumstances. But when I offered my opinion, he shook it off as unimportant and went ahead and did what he intended from the start. My voice was seldom heard when it came to the big decisions, and it took me a long time to find one with enough authority and volume for him to hear me.

Until today, I haven't shared with the world that I was once married to a minister, but only to a select few of people I trust. I guess I still suffer from a form of battle fatigue and carry the belief that people will judge me by who I was married to. When I do let out this bit of information, I usually experience a shocked look on the face of the person lucky enough to learn a little of my past. Over the years, it has gotten easier for me, and time really does heal.

The memories remain, though.

PART TWO

FISHBOWLS AND BIRDCAGES

ADJUSTING TO MY NEW LIFE

As I predicted, we moved to a new church after Chad graduated from theology school. Going through the process of learning what appointments were open within his salary range, going over the possibilities, and Chad's rejection of each one based on either something he'd heard from a fellow preacher or from some inner feeling he had, and looking at parsonages to see what they were like, were all exhausting for me.

It was amazing to me that he finally got a new assignment, and I thought if he had been less picky, we might have fared better in the long run. As it turned out, he had five choices and turned every one of them down, each for different reasons. How we ended up with a new appointment at all was a mystery to me. All I could think about through this entire dance was moving to a strange, new place, meeting a new congregation, and surviving another First Sunday.

As the years passed, and this pattern repeated itself every three or four years, it never got easier for me. It was during these periods that Chad was in his element, thriving over the discussions and deliberations of where his next appointment would be, meeting new people, showing me off to a new congregation. I think he felt in control during these negotiations, where he had the power to study potential parishes and then turn them down for reasons only he knew. Why he was so negative about potential assignments was something that I just couldn't understand. And he never shared this with me.

I was more concerned over neighborhoods, our future home, the number of children in the potential church, and public school districts. I wanted Dan and Kent to be happy wherever we were, and I wanted them to have a good education and close friends. I had already come to realize that what I desired for myself wasn't deemed important, so I focused on my boys with all of my comments and recommendations.

I packed boxes, cleaned parsonages, replaced stock curtains and rugs that I had put away for our time in the parsonage, and prepared myself for each new beginning. When Dan and Kent were small, they got into the excitement of packing; this attitude changed as they became teen-agers.

For the most part, I simply shut down emotionally during these periods of transition. I went through all of the required motions of going-away parties, new church interviews and parsonage tours, meeting the minister who was leaving the place we were going to, giving a tour of our home to the minister replacing Chad, and preparing myself for a new community and new people to get to know.

I didn't do a very good job, even with all the practice.

Including the student appointment, we lived in six parsonages before I finally made my last move out of parsonages forever. While very different, they all were also quite the same in many ways. Perhaps their similarities were based on the family that moved into each one. There were some that I liked better than others, and one that I truly hated. *Parsonage Green* greeted us everywhere.

Of the whole bunch, only one stands out in my memory as one that I would have liked to homestead in, and stay forever. Some were fishbowls; others were birdcages; a few were a combination of the two. In some, I could get out of from time to time and stretch my wings, while in others I felt like a fish, trapped and swimming in circles, forever looking through the glass, but not able to experience the outside world.

Parsonage life was definitely not for the faint of heart or thin-skinned.

It wasn't all bad. In fact, there were some great times, and I have memories and stories, actually more good than bad. As Chad and I moved through life together, we were a team, each propping up the other in areas where we were weak. For me, I was situated in the background, always trying to figure out this thing labeled *The Call* that was the mainstay of his life, while for him I was his chief cheerleader, encouraging him when he had challenges or got into tight spots with his congregation. It could be draining at times.

I was not cut out, and certainly not prepared, for this life, and Chad had his own ideas of the person he wanted me to be. I did my best for many years, as did Chad. I don't want to paint him with too harsh a brush, but there were some things that, as time went on, being revealed to me, caused me great personal anguish and unhappiness. Sometimes I look at our life as a jigsaw puzzle – some of the pieces fit very neatly and nicely, but those that didn't fit ruined the picture.

INDIAN CREEK

If I had thought that Pleasant Hill was rural, I had no idea of what rural really was until we drove into the Indian Creek community. The boys and I, in our small station wagon, followed Chad, driving a U-Haul truck. As we drove down the winding road into town, which actually was located along the shores of a pretty good-sized creek in the rolling hills piedmont region of Georgia, I had a sick feeling in my stomach, accentuated by passing a diamond-shaped caution sign, riddled with bullet holes, warning us of a hair-pin curve ahead.

It had been 20 miles since we had passed a town of any size, and I knew that we were all probably in for a good case of culture shock. It was not a good omen, as far as I could tell. The boys were asking question after question, to which I did my best in answering, while trying to keep a positive tone to my voice so as not to give away my illness and insecurities.

Running alongside of the creek was a railroad track, and after crossing the tracks into town, the church was easy to spot, with its parsonage sitting next to it, facing both the creek and tracks. Back behind the church was a factory of some kind – I would learn that it was a textile mill. It was a lovely little brick church with tall steeple, built in the early 1900's, and most of its members were either founding members or their descendants. Chad told me that the congregation totaled about 125 members, and I mused over how they would be able to pay his rookie minister salary.

The accompanying two-story parsonage was also brick, and I could see upon driving into town that it had a chimney, which meant it had a fireplace, something I had missed having at Pleasant Hill. Since this church wasn't one of his original five choices, I hadn't made an earlier trip to visit, and I had not seen the parsonage. All I had was a hand-drawn floor plan that the minister's wife mailed to me a couple of weeks before moving day, with a few comments about the temperamental heating system, a door handle that was finicky and hard to lock, and something about a memorial garden in the back yard.

Studying the crude floor plan, I had already determined which bedrooms would be the boys' and which one would be the master bedroom. Even with the nausea rolling around in my stomach, my curiosity reached a state of heightened awareness, and I was actually eager to step through the parsonage doors to see what our next home was going to be like.

Although I wasn't keen on going to a new church, my sense of adventure gave me strength., and curiosity got the better of me.

Pulling up into the parsonage driveway, I was surprised to see three white-haired ladies standing on the back stoop, waving to us. A welcoming committee! How different from our approach three years ago at Pleasant Hill. I pulled up behind the U-Haul, and the boys unlatched themselves from their car seats and bounded out of the car, excited to be the first ones inside the house. Chad jumped down from the cab of the truck, grabbed my hand, and together we walked up the walkway to greet our new parishioners.

All of my fear and nausea floated into the warm June sky the minute we were greeted by the three ladies standing on the back stoop. They called us out by name as we walked up to the house, and reached out their arms to give us a hug. Standing like stair steps, they introduced themselves as the Newsome Sisters - the tallest, and thinnest, was Lydia, the next in height was Judith, and the short round one was Ellie. Their excitement over our arrival was contagious, and they could hardly wait for us to go inside so that they could give us the grand tour. This was so very different from my Pleasant Hill experience, I relaxed and began looking forward to my new home.

Of all the parsonages we lived in, this one was my all-time favorite, due mostly to these three ladies and the pride that they took in the church's home. All three were members of the Parsonage Committee, and Ellie was on the Finance Committee. It didn't take me long to learn how to manipulate them to get almost anything that I wanted for the house.

"Come in, come in, let's show you the house," Lydia exclaimed as she opened the screen door leading into the small kitchen.

As we stepped inside, all three were almost dancing in delight at our surprise at seeing the kitchen table set with snacks of homemade cookies and freshly cut fruit, and a pitcher of cold lemonade, with four glasses already poured and waiting for us. Not at all like our arrival at Pleasant Hill. Dan and Kent swooped down on the plate of cookies, and I let them enjoy themselves without cutting them off after one cookie.

The sisters didn't let us sit down, but handed us each a glass. I grabbed a cookie, and followed them into the hallway leading to the rest of the house. Munching on the cookie, I didn't have to talk much or comment on what I was seeing. We followed them down the hall to see our new home.

It was an old house, and looked like it had been inspired by a Federal Four design, with obvious renovating and remodeling having been done sometime in the house's history. From the kitchen, which had been enlarged and remodeled at some point at the back of the house, a wide hallway led from it to the front door. It didn't take an instant to see that I would be living in another *Parsonage Green* home. On one side of the hallway was a living room, with fireplace, and dining room, and on the other side were an office, bathroom and bedroom. Upstairs had a similar central hallway. On one side was a bathroom and large bedroom, and on the other side were two bedrooms. In the full basement dwelled an ancient furnace that provided hot water heat for the radiators above and an equally prehistoric washing machine and dryer. I had noticed the radiators in every room, and mentally took note of the previous minister's wife's instructions about the heating system.

The furnishings were typical parsonage – vintage hand-me-downs, probably from parishioners' homes, and cheap-looking pieces from a local furniture store, perhaps. Like our previous home, it felt sterile to me, but I could see possibilities in this house becoming a home. There was something about it that felt good.

After a quick tour of our new home, we headed back to the kitchen, where Lydia and Judith were urging us to eat more snacks. Ellie had corralled Chad in the study, and with the door closed, I didn't know what they were talking about. I was feeling pretty comfortable, and liked these sisters immediately. Maybe my uneasy feelings were unwarranted. There was so much to learn about them and about Indian Creek, and this was only scratching the surface.

In a few minutes, Ellie and Chad emerged. I learned later that she hand delivered Chad's paycheck every month, and on moving day he got an advance in case we'd need it. The three sisters offered to help us unload the truck, but didn't hesitate to hastily excuse themselves and leave when we said that we could do it ourselves. They were too old to help much, but it was a friendly gesture.

Moving day was Thursday, the same as it had been three years earlier, which gave us two days to settle in and prepare ourselves for First Sunday. I wasn't happy about Chad's office being in the house, but there wasn't anything I could say about it. I hadn't been inside the church yet, and didn't know that every room in the church was being used for a specific purpose, so this was the only place that he could claim as his study. There would be a good bit for me to get used to with this arrangement.

I also was perturbed when I removed the temporary bedspreads that were on the beds for appearance sake. The mattresses were old and stained, and I almost got sick thinking about what germs were hiding there. I flipped the mattresses, only to find that the other sides were worse. I made a mental note to myself to campaign for new mattresses first chance I got. Sighing, I pulled out our mattress pads from the box of linens, covered the offending stains, made the beds, and tried not to think about them.

Other than those two things, I was pleased with the house, its roominess, and the furnishings, even though they were old and quite used. Dan and Kent each had a room of their own, which they were thrilled about, and they had a grand time unpacking their toys and making their new space their own. It wouldn't take me long to learn other things about our home, which weren't so ideal and most probably typical of an old house, but for that day I was content.

I discovered that the refrigerator was filled with several casserole dishes, a gallon of milk, a dozen eggs, a pound of bacon, and a loaf of bread. Our dinner and breakfast were taken care of for our first day in Indian Creek, and with the leftovers, for a few meals afterward. I anticipated a pounding, and was not disappointed. By the time the First Sunday was at an end, my freezer and cupboards were full. I didn't have to go out to find a grocery store for several days.

While I began unpacking boxes, Chad sequestered himself in his new office preparing his first sermon and unpacking his theology books.

THE NEWSOME SISTERS

As I remember the Newsome Sisters, a smile breaks out on my face. Sometimes I wonder if we had stayed at Indian Creek longer than Chad's stock three years, that life might have been different for me. I really don't know if it would have made a difference in the long run, but it might have helped me to deal with my role as a minister's wife. I wish I could have packed them up and moved them with us to each new home.

The ending probably would have been the same, because with each place we lived, nothing could change the fact that I was married to Chad, and he had his own ideas of who he wanted me to be as well as his own demons to fight. Indian Creek was a fishbowl in the truest sense of the image, but there was a friendly view looking out, even if the environment inside the fishbowl had its flaws.

Now that I am about the age that these three sisters were when I met them on the kitchen stoop of the parsonage, I appreciate them even more, and in many ways can identify with them. They were all single - old maids, spinsters – whatever the correct term is for three deeply southern, fiercely loyal, and strongly independent women who lived together in a delightful little bungalow and who, like me, were an enigma to the other residents of their little town. And, like me, they were eccentric, each one in her own delightful way. As I began my adventure of living alone, I often thought about the Newsome Sisters and patterned myself after them.

I remember one afternoon, sitting at the kitchen table having a cup of tea with Lydia. We were discussing the parsonage and its needs. The Parsonage Committee had a budget for improvements, and she wanted to know what we needed. New mattresses! It didn't bother me that we didn't have air-conditioning, a dishwasher, or that I didn't have a clue how hot water radiators worked. I wanted my family to sleep on fresh, new mattresses.

I confided to her how the stains sickened me, and that I didn't like sleeping on a mattress that another couple had used for their *intimate* moments. I also didn't like my boys sleeping on beds that other children had soiled. Lydia agreed with me, and wrote it down on her notepad.

From mattresses, our conversation drifted on to former pastors and their wives, and then to marriage in general. Out of curiosity, I asked her why neither she nor her sisters had never married.

"Oh," she answered. "Judith had a beau when she was young. He joined the Navy, and was killed in World War II. She never met anyone after him who could hold a candle to him. And as for Ellie, well, she was just too darned persnickety to fall in love. Nobody was ever good enough for her. And she was too stuck-up for most boys to even try to get close to her."

"But, what about you?" I ventured.

Lydia's mouth curved into a Mona Lisa smile, she put her hands together with the tips of her fingers touching, and gazed at them.

"Let's just put it this way," she said. "I was in love once, and thought it was forever. It wasn't. But I'll tell you one thing. If I had ever married, I couldn't have worn a white gown. It would have had to have a bit of lavender lace on it."

That was all she had to say about herself, and it was all I ever learned. Neither Judith nor Ellie would add anything whenever I pried them for information about Lydia's lost love. My imagination can take me there, and I understand.

I am now an avid Scrabble player, thanks in part to the Newsome Sisters. With dictionaries in hand, we'd compete at church game nights, and on occasion we'd slip a game in at their home when the boys and I would visit them.

Dan and Kent are fiercely competitive, also thanks to card games like Old Maid and Go Fish that the sisters taught them to play. The boys actually enjoyed playing these games more that I did, being the parsonage darlings that they were and the way they wiggled their way into the sisters' hearts. It was approved by Chad for the boys to go over to their house to play games or to stay with them if I needed a babysitter, while it wasn't suitable for me to make casual visits as the minister's wife. To Chad, it just wouldn't look right, and might lead others in the church to think that I was playing favorites. I had to sneak over there with my sons in tow whenever he was away, because he was right – they were my favorites.

It was an odd friendship. I loved the sisters dearly, but I never felt like I could confide in them, and they never asked anything personal or attempted to get to know me as anyone other than their minister's wife. Dan and Kent were more in their inner circle than I was, and I envied the closeness that grew between my sons and these ladies.

Like everyone, they grew to love Chad, and thought he hung the moon. There was no way I could let them know that things were less than perfect inside of the parsonage, or that I was always questioning what I was doing in the position I had found myself in as a preacher's wife. How could I confide in them, or in any church member for that matter, about all of the questions I had about God's calling or why he planted me in my particular flowerpot? I spent a lot of my time wondering if I was actually a Christian, since I had so many questions and no satisfactory answers.

The mattress incident was my first conscious attempt at manipulation, and it worked so well, I became very proficient at it. It wasn't two weeks after Lydia's and my kitchen conversation that we had brand new mattresses and box springs delivered to the parsonage. During the three years I lived in the parsonage, I used a similar method to get new carpeting in the living room and a new washer and dryer, as well as a few other minor repairs and updates to the house. I also learned to use this new talent on Chad, and while it wasn't 100 per cent effective, I laugh as I look back at how I got my way on some of my issues with him.

I wish the Newsome Sisters could be here in Wellspring with me now. I'm sure we'd be the grandest of friends. I can picture us sitting together on my porch, talking and laughing, playing a fierce game of Scrabble, well-worn dictionaries by our sides, challenging each other at every move. Of all the people I met during my years in parsonages, I think of them and miss them the most.

THE FISHBOWL

Indian Creek was a small community, bound together by the textile mill where many of our members worked, or were retired from, and the two churches in town, Southern Evangelical and Baptist. The church members believed that the minister and his family were exclusively theirs, and we enjoyed very little privacy.

The Newsome Sisters became my barometer or windsock of the feelings of the congregation, and I could always tell from the way they acted if something was brewing in the church. Judith knew everything that we did, and I often wondered if she might have binoculars at one of her windows where she could keep an eye on the parsonage and its family from across the creek. I learned very soon to always draw the window shades when it began to get dark, because she'd be checking on us to make sure we were OK. She knew if one of us were sick in the night. The next morning she'd be at our kitchen door.

"I saw your bathroom light on in the night. Is there anything I can do to help?"

Then, a little while later, Lydia would be at the door, apologizing for her sister's nosiness. At first, it annoyed me that we were being watched, but as I got to know the Newsome Sisters better, it grew to be a strange sort of security for me.

The pastor's study in the house became a tender spot. During the summer, with both boys underfoot, I stayed on pins and needles in an attempt to keep them away from the study door, especially if Chad had a church member with him, or if he was preparing his sermon for the following Sunday. He could get very cranky if we disturbed him or interrupted his meditation time, upsetting both me and the boys.

We spent most of our summer days at the community swimming pool, where the boys took lessons and learned to swim, and I kept my nose in a good novel. Occasionally, I'd enter into a conversation with one of the other moms, but for the most part they avoided me, not sure of what to talk about with the new preacher's wife.

I also had to learn not to answer the telephone, since our home line was Chad's office line, as well. Chad answered all of the phone calls during office hours, and I was only allowed to answer it in the evenings or if he wasn't home. The first summer there this wasn't a problem, since I didn't know anyone, but after awhile it became a source of contention between us when I would get a phone call while he was working in his study.

Since the study didn't have a separate entrance, people coming to see Chad would file through the kitchen in order to meet with him. Our front door was hardly ever used, since the driveway and parking area were at the back of the house.

If I didn't have the door latched, church members took the liberty to come right into the house without knocking. At first, I was startled to see people walking through my house, but as time went by, I became accustomed to it. I always made sure the door was locked every night, or I might find someone seated at my kitchen table the next morning waiting for Chad to come downstairs. I had no privacy, and was feeling more and more like a mere shadow. On more than one occasion, I'd be working in the kitchen when someone would come in, and never even greet me with a friendly "Hello," while passing through.

One morning Chad got into a heated argument with one of the church leaders while I was in the kitchen cleaning up the breakfast dishes, and Kent was sitting at the table finishing off a piece of cinnamon toast. I could tell things weren't going very well, because normally I could only hear the buzz of conversations drifting from the study, but voices were getting louder and some obscenities were flung at my husband.

Before I could make a hasty exit from the kitchen with Kent, Mr. Mason, the chairman of the Pastor-Parish Committee stomped across the floor, barely seeing me standing at the sink, my arms elbow-deep in dishwater, and slammed the kitchen door behind him as he headed out.

With his quick glance in my direction, a stricken look crossed his face, as he realized that both me and my son had probably heard what was said. Chad was at his heels, getting the door slammed in his face, and followed Mr. Mason into the yard.

I couldn't imagine what the problem might be. We hadn't been at Indian Creek but a couple of months, and Chad hadn't had time to anger anyone, as far as I knew. I watched through the kitchen window as Chad caught up with him, calmed him down, and the two of them stood out there for several minutes discussing something and finally shaking hands. Whatever crisis it was, it had passed, except for the fact that I had witnessed the entire thing. Chad stomped back into the house.

"What was that all about?" I asked him as he tromped through the kitchen, ignoring me.

Chad retreated into his office, closing the door behind him, indicating to me that there would be no conversation about this. He didn't come out for a couple of hours. I was smart enough not to question him further about what had transpired. As for Mr. Mason, he never looked me straight in the eyes after that morning, and I always felt that he went out of his way to avoid speaking to me.

THE MEMORIAL GARDEN

Once we were settled in and First Sunday was behind us, I began to explore the yard. It was woefully lacking in landscaping, but I could see where a previous minister's wife had planted daffodils and other perennial flowers around the borders of the walkways.

I also investigated a flower garden that was badly neglected. The only way I could tell that it was a garden and not simply an area that hadn't seen a lawn mower in a long time was the black metal garden plaque that stuck up from amid the weeds. It was one of those that you'd find in every cheap mail order catalog that finds its way to your mailbox, and it had faded with the years. Its words, *Mine is a Garden of Hope,* could hardly be deciphered. I wanted to get in there and clean it up, but to Chad it was smack in the way of his lawnmower path, and with the first lawn haircut, all evidence of any flowers ever having grown there was gone. He tossed the plaque into the shrubbery next to the back porch, so that it wouldn't get caught in the mower blades.

He then leveled the daffodil rows, and since the greenery wasn't left long enough after the spring blooms, the daffodils died and didn't come back the next year. I wanted to plant a flower garden, but Chad was adamant about his yard being neat, and didn't want anything to get in his way when he was grooming the grass. Sadly, I settled for a couple of flower boxes that I picked up at the local hardware store, and the boys and I planted a few marigolds in them and set them on the back stoop.

It was the following week after Chad's first lawn mowing exercise that Mr. Mason visited him in his study and lost his cool with my husband. It seemed that the bunch of weeds with the garden plaque was the *Annie May Memorial Garden*, and had been there since her death 20 years previously. While it wasn't the minister's responsibility to tend the garden, it also wasn't his job to destroy it.

Somewhere tucked away in the back of my mind was the note from my predecessor about a memorial garden, but it hadn't registered that this pile of weeds was holy ground. I didn't say anything to Chad about it – I decided I was better off to stay silent about what I knew.

Of course, the Newsome Sisters got into the fracas over the *Annie May Memorial Garden* being destroyed. They thought the entire episode was hilarious, especially Judith, who wasn't as serious as her two sisters, and who had a lively sense of humor. All three of them shouldered some of the guilt over the entire matter for not telling us about the garden when we moved in, which greatly helped matters with the church in general. For the most part, the only people concerned about it were the descendants of Miss Annie, but they had seemed to lack any interest in maintaining the garden, from what Judith informed me.

Judith told me, "You'd think her children and grandchildren would care more about her than to let her garden grow up in weeds. But then, they never were very kind to her while she was alive. What Chad did probably was a favor to them."

"Who was she, anyhow?" I asked.

"Oh, she was one of the best Sunday School teachers the church ever had and the kindest lady to ever live in this town. Every child who grew up in Indian Creek either went through her third grade class or were taught by her in Vacation Bible School," Judith told me. "She was an angel if there ever was one and was loved by everyone in town. It's too bad that her own family never appreciated everything that she did for others or the wonderful influence she had on all the children in town."

"But, why was the Memorial Garden planted in the parsonage back yard?" I inquired.

"There was a huge disagreement about the use of the church grounds," Judith said. "Some of the members didn't feel like it was fair to memorialize one person and not another. The preacher's wife at the time was friends with Miss Annie, and volunteered the parsonage yard for the garden. It made sense, and solved the dilemma. At first, the children of the church took care of the garden, but over the years, memories faded, new ministers came and went, and the garden was all but forgotten. That is, until Chad mowed it down."

"I'm so sorry that this has happened to revive so many awful feelings," I said.

"Don't worry about it for a minute, Fran," Judith answered. "I have a plan. It will all be just fine."

At the next Administrative Board meeting, Judith suggested that the church purchase a living Christmas tree for the parsonage that year which could be planted on the church grounds after the holidays in memory of Miss Annie. Everyone agreed that this was a good idea, mainly because it didn't involve a lot of work on anyone's part. And so it was that we had a lovely six-foot fir tree in our home that December, which later graced the church lawn. A descriptive plaque was created by one of the church members and placed at the foot of the tree that clearly stated that Annie May was memorialized by the tree.

Chad was totally unrepentant about the entire episode, and took on a victim's mantle, which he wore splendidly. I don't think Mr. Martin ever quite recovered from being caught by me for his temper tantrum in the parsonage, although in time most people took up the humor of the Newsome Sisters and the story grew to be one of Indian Creek's urban legends. I was questioned about it several years later by the minister's wife who was living there at the time, and I hardly recognized the story, it had been embellished so much.

CHAD'S DEMANDS

Once summer was over, Dan was off to first grade, and Kent was enrolled in the Baptist Church's preschool every morning. For the first time in five years I didn't have a child to hide behind, and I was at loose ends for something to keep me busy. I joined a morning circle, which met once a month, but other than that I had no responsibilities. Thankfully, the weekly bulletin was taken care of by a volunteer church member, and all I had to do was proofread Chad's terrible spelling and walk his weekly information across the church parking lot on Wednesday morning to the volunteer of the day.

It was during these fall days that Chad decided that I would become his silent partner in ministry. He wanted me to go with him to visit church members, make hospital visits, and check in with the community's funeral home to see if anyone needed ministerial comfort. About three mornings each week after the boys were safely deposited in their respective schools, we would head out to see those people whom Chad had determined needed our visit.

We'd always be back by lunchtime in time for Kent to come home from preschool, after which Chad would take off again to visit church members he felt didn't need a visit from me. I didn't know how he made his list to decide – he reminded me of Santa Claus determining who was naughty and who was nice. I'm not sure if I had the pleasure of visiting the nice ones or the naughty. For the most part, I enjoyed the mornings that we made visits, and I met some pretty amazing people during these trips. I also looked forward to the afternoons when he was gone – I never got used to him having his office in the house, and it was during these afternoon hours that I could enjoy time with my sons, or by myself in quiet solitude.

Chad was purposely in charge during our morning visits. He dominated the conversation, and I usually sat quietly listening, smiling, and nodding my head. Every now and then I'd take someone's hand to hold it, especially when it was a condolence call or a hospital visit. I never was sure why he wanted me with him, but I suspected that he simply wanted to know where I was, and that was the easiest way for him to keep up with my whereabouts.

Chad had begun showing signs of paranoia, thinking that I was talking about him whenever I was with a group of other women or at a Bible Study or circle meeting. I would get a grilling from him upon returning home, wanting to know who I was with, what we talked about, and whether I said anything about him. I never did, even though after several years there were times when I was dying to share my feelings with someone else. It was easier for him to have me with him where he didn't have to worry about what I might be saying.

Another one of Chad's ways of getting me involved in his ministry was the way he'd volunteer me for jobs. During board meetings, if nobody was nominated to take on a church position, he'd volunteer me, never asking me first. During my first year at Indian Creek I became a Sunday School teacher for the adult couples' class, served as the counselor for the youth group, joined the adult choir, and was superintendent of Vacation Bible School. I complained to him that I didn't appreciate being handed jobs that nobody in the church wanted.

He just laughed at me and said, "Well, Fran, I know you'd never volunteer on your own to do anything, so it's up to me to do it for you."

I let him get away with this at Indian Creek, but I learned to put my foot down - for the most part - at subsequent appointments and only take jobs that I wanted.

Even though I had not volunteered on my own to sing in the choir, this job became one that I really liked, and I continued singing in church choirs at each church we served. I had never sung alto, but the choir needed one, so there I was, learning to sing harmony for the first time in my life. I sat next to Judith Newsome, a strong singer who I could follow very easily. Ellie and Lydia offered to sit with Dan and Kent during the church services, so I would sit up in the choir loft and watch my small sons wiggling in the pew while the two sisters kept them entertained with toys they'd pull out of their purses at key times. I doubt if any of them ever paid much attention to Chad's sermons, but they sure had a good time in church together. Every Sunday, the boys would come home smelling of Lydia's Estee Lauder perfume from all the loving they'd gotten from her during church.

I also looked forward to Wednesday night choir practice, when Chad would watch the boys, put them into the tub and then to bed. It was the only time I ever got a break from the evening routine at home.

On the intimate side of things, there were some changes in Chad's behavior and needs that puzzled me. Daily sex was not part of our schedule anymore, although we still made love on a regular basis, several times a week, although I hesitated to call it *making love*. It seemed very impersonal to me. Soon after we moved to Indian Creek, he decided that he wanted to try different positions for our lovemaking, and from that time on, we never had sex face-to-face, but in positions that were less intimate. Sometimes I felt like I wasn't even present during those interludes.

He also began some other weird habits that I didn't like. For some reason, he became a sort of exhibitionist. He got a big kick out of unzipping his pants in public places and exposing himself. This happened mainly in elevators, and I grew to dread our visits to hospitals, because if there were no other people in the elevator car with us, this became something I could almost count on. He seemed to enjoy my shock and panic at this little activity, along with my anxiety over him tucking himself back in before the door opened at the next floor. I asked him time and again to stop, but he would only laugh, enjoying every moment of my reaction.

Sometimes he'd grab me and try to fondle me, either my breasts or crotch, in public areas – again, elevators were among his places of choice. I thought it was all very immature and adolescent, and why he was did this was more than I could understand.

At home, Chad liked to have sex in places that I didn't consider private. Some nights he would awaken me, and lead me by the hand outdoors to a blanket in the yard or to a lawn chair on the porch, where we'd have a "quickie." To Chad, this activity was exciting and daring. For me, it was nerve-wracking.

It was at these times that I began to find my voice, and it was not one of approval. Chad brushed off my objections as me just being silly.

There was a lot I didn't understand, but having no other sexual experience except with him, I thought that probably all men must be like this, seeming to always have their attention on their private parts and their manhood. Having no one to talk to about this, I kept it all to myself, and gritted my teeth whenever he'd do something I considered peculiar. It was still pretty weird, no matter how I looked at it.

LOOKING BACK AND ROCKING ALONG

One of the chairs in my living room is the one that Chad gave me for my thirtieth birthday. When he gave it to me, I was hurt and offended. I felt like he was making fun of my advancing age. I love it now, and find it very comfortable and rock-able, and am glad that I have it. I'm not sure why I kept the thing. When I left the parsonage, I didn't take much with me. Of course, my beloved pecan table went with me, along with the rocking chair. When you live in a furnished parsonage, there isn't much to carry out.

I remember that birthday vividly. I woke up early in the morning, following one of Chad's middle-of-the-night interruptions to my sleep, went through the motions of getting the boys up and ready for school, watched Dan get onto the school bus, and walked Kent to the car when the carpool mom of the day drove up to get him. Chad hadn't said anything to me about my birthday, and I sat at the kitchen table nursing a cup of coffee and feeling very sorry for myself. My parents had sent me a birthday card with a check for $25 in it – enough for me to buy something for myself to wear, and I had talked to them on the phone the previous evening. Other than that, it felt like my birthday was going unnoticed.

Chad came out of his office after the boys were gone, and I thought we were going to be heading out on our regular morning visits. Instead, he asked me to go into town to the post office to pick up our mail. This was a job that he usually did, but I was happy to get out of the house for a few minutes. It was a brisk March day, and the five-minute walk up the hill into town lifted my spirits. When I returned, I heard him calling me from the living room to come in to look at something. There he was, standing and grinning next to a new rocking chair, with a big pink bow wrapped around its back.

"Happy 30th Birthday, Fran," Chad beamed. He put his hand on the back of the chair, causing it to rock back and forth. "Do you like it?"

It was all I could do not to break out in tears, I was so devastated. I forced a smile, saying, "It's beautiful, Chad. Thank you."

He could see that I wasn't pleased, and didn't know what to do or say. I mumbled something about what a nice gesture it was, hugged and kissed him, and sat down on it to try it out. I remember feeling very old that morning.

Now, as I sit in the same old chair, I don't feel old at all, and certainly don't feel like I've aged as much as it has. It is banged up from numerous moving vans and trucks, and the finish has worn down to the original wood color on the arms. The stenciled design on the back has faded to where it is hard to see what it was when it was new, and the rockers are covered with knicks and scratches, mainly from Martin and Coretta attacking them while I rock.

I see myself at age 30, thinking my life had little meaning or purpose, and still asking myself what I was doing in the role of a minister's wife. Nothing in the few years Chad had been a minister had made me feel any better about it, and the chair became a symbol to me of who I wasn't. I hardly ever sat in the chair while we were married, yet I was compelled to pack it into the truck when I moved out for the last time.

It's amazing how a simple chair could become such a focal point in my life through all the many changes over the years. It has become a kind of symbol for *bloom where you are planted*. Wherever I've been in my life, this danged chair has been with me!

I can also still hear Lydia proclaim when she saw the chair for the first time, "Is he out of his mind? How could he have done that to you on such a milestone birthday! Somebody needs to have a talk with that boy."

And, thanks to her, it wasn't long before everyone in the church knew about my new rocking chair and my 30th birthday. The next Sunday at church, I received many knowing nods and empathetic pats on my back as I was wished a belated happy birthday.

I am also reminded of other gifts Chad gave to me over the years. Never one to be nostalgic or sentimental, my gifts were mostly things that he could use. Most of them stayed in the parsonage when I moved out – the electric frying pan, the vacuum cleaner, the handy-dandy vegetable slicer and dicer. Chad was always a sucker for gimmicks, and I was the recipient of many of his purchases. I also have four identical pairs of earrings that he gave me over the years – my birthstone, aquamarine, studs. He never remembered that he had already given me the same pair on an earlier birthday or Christmas. One of these days, I'll disperse these to my granddaughter, if I ever have one, and to my great-nieces.

I am just happy that I am able to smile now about these things.

FRIENDSHIPS AMONG MINISTERS

While at Indian Creek, we became friends with Joe and Lori Carter, a clergy couple about our age who had three daughters. Lori was the daughter of a preacher, so she had no problems whatsoever with the life she had, and unlike me, who questioned everything, she had a simple faith and felt that she was called to be a minister's wife. Joe was a go-getter. He was minister of one of the largest churches in our district, and he had his eyes on the Clergy Superintendent job within the next few years. A ladder-climber, he was political to the *nth* degree.

Chad and Joe hit it off immediately upon meeting at a district social event for ministers and their spouses, which surprised me, because Chad always appeared so distant around other men. There was something about Joe that appealed to Chad, I supposed.

I liked Lori from the moment I met her, and turned to her when I had questions or problems about our church. She was the closest thing I had to a friend during those three years, and truth be told, I never had a friend like her for the rest of the time I spent as a minister's wife.

Their daughters' ages were sandwiched between Dan and Kent's, and even though they were girls, the five kids always got along and had lots of fun when we got together.

Lori didn't have a job outside of her home, but devoted all of her time to her daughters and to her calling in the church. I thought I was busy in our church with the jobs Chad had dumped into my lap, but she was twice as busy in hers. Of course, being a larger church, there was more going on during the week, so there were many more opportunities for her to be involved. We didn't get together very often, but we became great phone buddies, and when our husbands were away at their church functions, Lori and I spent many hours chatting on the phone.

Joe convinced Chad that he, too, was Clergy Superintendent material, and gave him advice on how to work the system and move up in the church. The two of them began going on retreats together, where they took courses in church management and other church-related skills, and Joe coached Chad on how to "work" the board and church leaders to get what he wanted.

They also began playing golf and going fishing together. Joe had a little fishing boat that he named *Visitation*. That way, when someone in the church needed him for something, his secretary could truthfully say that he was out on visitation. I thought this was pretty corny, yet funny in a way. It was my belief that Joe was as full of hot air as he was information of any value, and for a minister, he seemed to be pretty full of himself. Chad thought Joe had all the answers, citing him as the authority whenever anything came up that I didn't understand. Joe became Chad's mentor for being a successful pastor.

I liked Joe just fine, but I never quite trusted him. There seemed to be something phony about him that I couldn't put my finger on. And I wondered about his and Lori's relationship. They appeared to be a loving couple, but Lori never said anything to me indicating that she really loved Joe or missed him when he and Chad were off somewhere together. I dismissed it as my own misgivings about Chad and me that I was reflecting onto her.

We stayed in touch with Joe and Lori – or rather, Joe and Chad stayed in touch - even after each of our husbands moved on to other churches. Joe moved up to a larger church, while Chad's next move was a lateral one - not much bigger than Indian Creek, but less rural, which I guessed was a promotion. I began to lose faith that the Clergy Superintendent path was in the cards for Chad. Chad and Joe continued to go together to retreats and church meetings together.

But Lori and I didn't continue our friendship the way our husbands did – she was busy with her role as preacher's wife and mother like I was, and we didn't keep up with each other as closely as we had when we lived closer to one another. Besides, talking on the phone involved a long-distance call, and I didn't have it in my budget to indulge in such an extravagance.

THE MINISTER'S WIVES' GRAPEVINE

Part of the Southern Evangelical Church was an attempt to bring pastors and their wives together on a regular basis. The life of a minister and family could be very isolated, as I was experiencing with each church and community.

Every month, the ministers in our district met to discuss the latest developments within the Church, and to take part in a continuing education program. While they were doing whatever it was that ministers did when they got together, the wives would meet for a short program, sharing time, and enjoying refreshments. I really didn't like going to these meetings, but Chad felt that it was important for me to become more visible within the church political structure, and he especially wanted me to chum up with the Clergy Superintendent's wife.

His strategy didn't work in that area, mainly because the Superintendent's wife had a job and hardly ever attended the meetings, but I did learn an awful lot from listening to the other wives' stories about what was going on in their churches and in their personal lives.

There was always chitchat about parsonages, fishbowls, and birdcages. Because we, as preachers' wives, didn't feel comfortable confiding in church members about things that went on in our personal lives or with our minister husbands, these meetings allowed us to vent with one another. Most of the time, it seemed little more than bitching and gossip to me, but on one occasion, my ears perked up when a discussion arose about a minister who had died suddenly, and how his family was now being moved out of their parsonage.

"Poor June. I don't know how she is coping or what she is going to do," I overheard one wife say to another while helping herself to a doughnut at the refreshment table. "She has to be out of the parsonage by the first of next month."

"I know. It's terrible just thinking about it," commented her conversation buddy. "That's exactly why I told Tom that I want to buy a condo or something of our own as soon as we can. We need to have a place we can call our own."

My curiosity got the best of me. "Who are you talking about? What happened?" I asked, doing my best to enter their conversation, without appearing to butt in.

"Didn't you hear?" Wife No. 1 asked. "Howard Markman, over at White Springs, had a massive heart attack and died – right there on the golf course - with his lay leader standing next to him when it happened."

"No. I didn't know him." I said. "But why does his wife have to move out of their house?" I was still considered a newbie in this new realm of life, and there was a lot yet for me to learn.

"They've already appointed Robert Thomas, the associate pastor at First Church in Madison to replace him," chimed in Wife No. 2. "June and the kids have to move out of the parsonage, so that the Thomas' can move in. Nobody seems to know what June is going to do."

"That's horrible!" I exclaimed, probably louder than I should have. I was shocked. How could the church be so callous? "Is anyone doing anything to help her?" I questioned.

Wife No. 1 shrugged and looked at me with a knowing, *welcome to our world* look. "You have a lot to learn, Sweetie," she said, as she took a bite of her doughnut and smiled sympathetically.

I was stunned. As the two wives continued their conversation, I casually meandered over to another group of women who were talking about the local school system. But I couldn't get poor June out of my mind.

I later learned that in the case of a minister's death, a new one was appointed by the church conference as soon as possible. The widow and children of the deceased minister would have to vacate the parsonage immediately, usually within 90 days. I also learned that the church made no provision for helping the family find a new home.

For a grieving widow, this could be devastating, especially if she didn't have a career or means of supporting herself. The minister's insurance package, I was told by a veteran wife, wasn't worth "a hill of beans."

The one thing that hit me like a slap in the face was learning how fast the church acted in events like Howard Markman's death. I couldn't believe that the church could be so cruel.

I knew that Chad had a pension and a life insurance policy through the church, but I didn't know how much either was worth. After hearing about the Markmans, I began to worry about myself and my children.

When I asked Chad about it, he snapped at me, "What, Fran? Are you thinking about knocking me off? Do you think I won't provide for my family?"

I immediately apologized, saying, "I'm sorry for asking," over and over again, until he finally got over it.

I never asked again. But I began scheming.

I decided that I needed to either find a job, go back to school, or both. If the church wasn't going to look after my best interests, and if Chad didn't take this seriously, I determined to put myself into a position of being able to take care of myself.

I couldn't do anything while living in Indian Creek, but I could certainly let my opinions be known when it came time for our next move.

MANIPULATION AND ACCUSATION

As our third year at Indian Creek progressed, Chad began showing signs of restlessness. I knew he would be asking for a transfer the coming summer. I took a more active part in his decision this time, mainly because I had a hidden agenda for myself.

Both boys were now in school full days, and I wanted to either get a job or go back to school myself. I even went behind Chad's back and spoke to our Clergy Superintendent about my wants. He understood my needs, having a wife who was a professional teacher, and promised me that he would do his best to steer Chad in a direction that would be good for me, as well as for him.

The same old pattern began to repeat itself. Whatever the Clergy Superintendent suggested to Chad, he would find something wrong with it. I was getting pretty antsy about the whole thing, because not only did I have the boys to think about – their new school, neighborhood, and home, but I also wanted to live in a town that had things that I needed. I had to trust that our Clergy Superintendent would intervene on my behalf.

One of the things I did to get ready for this dream of change in my life was to get my parents on my side. My father and mother were proud beyond words that their daughter was married to a minister, and they felt very strongly that I should sacrifice any personal wants for the better good of my husband's calling. This made it very tough on me, because I didn't dare complain to them or gripe about anything that was going on in my life. My dad had quit encouraging me to go back to school to get my degree, and was now encouraging me to be the best minister's wife there had ever been. It was a tall order for me to get them to change their perspective on things.

I did this through my newly found skill of manipulation. I had all of my reasons and arguments lined up in order in my mind as I approached Chad with my idea.

First, I convinced him that I needed a short vacation, and that it had been over three years since I had been to see my parents. I emphasized that the boys probably would enjoy a road trip with their mom, where they wouldn't have church people hovering over them all of the time. I gently reminded him that our planned trip home at Christmastime had been cancelled due to the death of one of our church members. While Chad most certainly couldn't take time off at this time of year – when appointments were being made – it would be a good time for me to take the boys away for a few days.

My parents had moved to Florida when my dad retired while Chad was in Theology School, and a winter trip down south would be good for us all. And while we were there, I knew my dad would take us all to Disney World and Epcot, which would be an educational adventure for our small sons.

Surprise of surprises, Chad thought this was a great idea, and began mapping out my trip for me with the dates I planned to be away. We decided that a week's trip would be long enough, and mid-March would be a good time to travel – it would even coincide with the boys' spring break, so they wouldn't miss any school days.

Now I had to plot my speech to my parents. As I drove with Dan and Kent down I-75 into Florida, I memorized what I planned to say. My emphasis would be on the information I had learned about the fate of a minister's widow, should something catastrophic happen to her husband. I certainly wouldn't want to have to move my little family into my parents' home. I needed to have something of my own that I could use to support us if something unexpected should happen to Chad.

With all of this whirling around in my mind, and with having to keep Dan and Kent happily occupied during the daylong trip, I also began feeling a huge sense of freedom. In some ways, I felt like a fish who had escaped the fishbowl, floundering and gasping for breath. But in another strange and uplifting way, I was a bird let out of a birdcage, testing my wings on this little independent jaunt, and feeling the glory of being away from the confines of the church and the parsonage.

This was the first time in our marriage that I had taken off on my own. I purposefully pushed the panic from my mind, and began thinking positively about the week in front of me.

The visit with my parents was wonderful. As I predicted, my dad took us all to Walt Disney World, where I enjoyed watching my little boys' faces more than I did the Magic Kingdom. My mom cooked for us, read to the boys, and generally pampered me. By mid-week I was ready to talk to them.

Armed with information, I laid out the facts about parsonage life and how it would end if I should find myself alone in the world. My parents, also armed, but with more misinformation than facts, couldn't believe that the church could be so callous.

It took some doing, but I finally got through to them, and once I did, they were solidly in my corner. The pedestal that they had put Chad up on when he went into the ministry wasn't quite as solid or high as it once was, and they began thinking, like me, that I needed to make some preparations on my own.

My dad offered to help me with tuition, if I should decide to go back to school. His rationalization: "Fran, we always intended to put you through college.

When you dropped out of school to get married, that didn't end our commitment. Whatever you need, you just ask us."

My mother chimed in with, "Don't forget your first obligation is to your family. But we trust you to do what you need to do to take care of yourself," she added as a side note.

I assured them that I would never compromise my job as wife and mother, but that it meant the world to me for them to understand my side of things.

About the time I was convincing my parents, Chad began phoning their home to make sure I was there and asking to talk to me. If I happened to be gone somewhere with the boys, he grilled whichever parent answered the phone about my whereabouts, how long I'd been gone, and when I'd be back. When I got on the phone with him, he insisted on an accounting of every minute of the day, and asked me if I'd seen anyone besides my parents that day.

My mother was appalled that he did this and pulled me aside the afternoon before we were to return home and asked, "Is there is a reason we should know about for Chad not to trust you? Is there something you need to tell me?"

I assured her, "No, Mom, I don't know why he's doing this. I guess he's just missing us – we've never been away from him." I didn't believe my answer to her, but I didn't have a good explanation for myself, either.

Upon arriving home from my expedition, I was greeted at the door by my husband, who pulled me into his office and shut the door, leaving the boys out in the hall, oblivious to what was going on.

 "OK, Fran, tell me the truth. Did you sleep with anyone while you were gone?"

"What are you talking about?" I was blindsided by his question.

"I just want the truth. Did you meet someone down there?"

"No, I didn't," I stammered, not believing Chad had asked this. "What would make you think such a thing?"

"I don't know," he admitted. "It was just that while you were gone, I had lots of time to think."

"Well, don't think anymore," I retorted. "And don't ever accuse me of something like that again."

I was angry, and stomped out of his office. What was going on? He had encouraged me to make the trip. Why would he accuse me of such a thing, and why would he harass my parents over the phone while I was at their house? It felt like he was intentionally trying to plant doubts in their minds about me, while imagining that I was not being faithful to him. I didn't have an answer.

This conversation stayed with me for awhile, and bothered me, but soon I was squarely back in reality, planning for another move. I actively became part of the process, and voiced my opinions, for the first time, in another next step in our lives.

Our Clergy Superintendent had pulled some strings to open up a position for Chad in a moderate sized town that also had a small state college in it. There would be plenty of opportunities for me to find a job if I wanted, as well as continue my education if I so desired. At first, Chad balked at this offer, but I used every ounce of convincing talent in my body to point out all the good things about it, and also played to his common sense that he shouldn't look a gift horse from the Clergy Superintendent in the mouth.

Joe even got into the act and convinced Chad into accepting the appointment. It was all set. We were heading for Mooresville, home of Georgia Central College and Broad Street Southern Evangelical Church.

MOVING AND PACKING, DÉJÀ VU ALL OVER AGAIN

I had a love-hate relationship with packing and moving. On one hand, I anticipated the move and had daydreams of new friends and people who would treat me as an individual and not an extension of Chad. On the other hand, I dreaded moving, knowing that probably things would be very similar – same song, different verse. The one thing that kept me going was a healthy dose of hope. That, and my commitment to provide my two sons with a good upbringing, and to live up to God's calling, which I was growing less and less sure of.

In my own home now, surrounded by evidence that I am a person in my own right, all of this history seems like a distant dream, now shrouded in foggy memories. I have no plans to move again, and hope that my next move will be when my ashes are cast across my vegetable garden by happy party-goers.

While some events remain crystal clear in my mind, many of the details of each move have blended together into one long shudder as I see myself in my memory becoming more and more invisible. Each move taught me lessons that have proved to be valuable in my life, but I can't shake the feelings I'd have every time we had to make a move. Indian Creek was the best of all the places and parsonages we lived in, and even with its faults, I look back at those three years with fondness. It was there that I began becoming aware of who I was and of the confines of being a minister's wife, or rather Chad's wife.

And it was there that I set my personal path for fishbowl and birdcage survival.

When I talk to Kent and Dan about their memories, I am amazed at the insight they had, even when they were young. They tell me now that they hated moving, and always felt at odds in each new parsonage until they could make a few friends and get all of their personal stuff strewn around their personal space.

With each move, they knew that it would only be for a few years, so they never got attached to their home and found it difficult to make lasting friends. They didn't really know what it felt like to be "at home." I am also surprised to hear that they knew from the time they were school age that something wasn't right between Chad and me, and that I didn't fit into the parsonage life. They sensed something was amiss long before I did. Kent even tells me that he felt a strong sense to protect me – of what he didn't know as a child. He has always been closely attuned to my feelings.

Every time the boys and I get together, something new comes out in our conversations about the past. When my marriage ended, I felt enormous guilt about failing God and the church, anger about secrets I had sworn to keep, and a belief that if I had been different or had handled things another way, everything would have come out o.k.

It is reassuring to me now to talk to my sons and learn that they weren't completely in the dark, and supported me the entire time. I look at them, seeing both their father and myself in their faces, and know that their DNA is the best of the two of us.

I am very thankful.

BROAD STREET CHURCH

Another three years in another church. In many ways Broad Street Southern Evangelical Church was a carbon copy of Pleasant Hill and Indian Creek, yet it was during these three years that I made my move and set my path as a potentially independent woman.

I won't go into great detail about the parsonage, except that this was the worst one we ever lived in. I detested it. Again, *Parsonage Green* greeted us as we moved in. What I disliked most about this place was its remoteness to any neighbors, the tiny rooms and cramped living space, and having only one bathroom for our growing family of four. Its only redeeming factors in my view were four huge pecan trees in the front yard, which provided us with nuts two of the three years we were there, and three sets of new mattresses and box springs. Someone must have heard that I was coming!

While Broad Street Church was located in town, the parsonage was two miles away, set on the main highway leading toward Macon, and our closest neighbor was almost a half mile away. The house had belonged to a church member who left it to the church when he died. Rather than sell the home, the church decided to use it as the parsonage. It didn't meet the Southern Evangelical Church requirements for parsonages, but evidently nobody had complained about it, so nothing had been done.

The church itself was fine, as far as churches go. I found the parishioners tolerant of me, and adoring of Chad, especially the women - no changes there. By this time, I had become adjusted to playing second fiddle to him, and having him being the topic of conversation whenever anyone found themselves in a position of having to talk to me.

I really liked the fact that Chad had an office in the church. I'm sure he liked it too, because he didn't spend much time at home. Joe had been assigned to a large church in Macon, thirty miles away, and the two of them remained very close friends. I didn't get to see Lori any more, and we hardly ever took the time to talk on the phone.

Of course there were church members that I liked better than others. My favorite was a man of about fifty years of age, who was mentally challenged and still lived with his mother, a plump, happy, and friendly white haired lady. Marvin had the intellect of - I'd say - an eight-year-old, and his mother, Hilda, made great use of her broom to discipline her six-foot-tall middle-aged little boy. They lived on the same highway as we did, and often when I'd drive by their home, I'd see Hilda running across her yard, chasing Marvin, her broom waving in the air above her head as she tried to catch him to give him a wallop.

Marvin took an immediate liking to me, and I always thought it amusing that the one person in all of the churches we served who truly loved me was this man-child. I made the mistake of referring to Chad as a turkey one day in Marvin's presence, responding to someone about something that Chad had done or said. *He's just an old turkey* made it to Marvin's ears that day.

Every week at church he'd seek me out and ask me in his booming voice, "Where's that old turkey of yours?"

We'd both laugh and I'd tell him that Chad was teaching Sunday School, preparing for his sermon, or whatever popped into my mind at the time.

Marvin was a hoot. He phoned the parsonage one summer evening, and while talking to me there was a flash of lightning and loud crash of thunder from an approaching storm. The power went off at both our houses.

"I have to go now, Miss Fran," he said. "I can't see you anymore." With that he hung up, leaving me laughing over the abruptness of the end to our conversation.

Kent and Dan loved Marvin, too, and considered him an over-sized playmate.

I made a true enemy one night at a church supper when Mr. Truman Cooper, the chairman of the Administrative Board sat across from me at the long table. He slammed down his empty iced tea glass on the table, and demanded, "Fran, go get me a refill of tea."

The boys and I had just sat down with our dinners, and had begun eating. I was startled by this outburst, and retorted, "Mr. Cooper, you can get up and get your own tea. I'm taking care of my children right now." I didn't intend to be short with him, but it surely came out that way.

He shouted, "You're nothing but one of those women's libbers! I hope you don't let your high-handed ways rub off on Mildred." With that, meek little Mildred, who resembled Olive Oyl in the Popeye cartoons, leaped up from her seat at the next table, grabbed his glass and scurried to fill up his glass of tea.

Chad jumped all over me when we got home that night for not doing what Mr. Cooper asked, but I stood my ground saying, "I'm not going to be someone's waitress. I don't care who Truman Cooper is."

The following day Chad told me that Mr. Cooper came to tell him that he needed to gain better control over his wife and family. Not only had he complained about the incident the night before, but he made a comment that I was nothing but a snob.

Chad let me know in no uncertain terms that I'd better start being nicer to the church members. I promised him I'd do my best, but I wasn't brave enough to tell Chad how the episode had upset me. Instead of speaking out, I silently made a point to never sit near Truman Cooper at any church activity.

After that, I knew beyond a shadow of a doubt that we'd be moving at the end of three years. I had a lot to accomplish in that short time.

GOING TO SCHOOL AND GETTING A JOB

What I loved about Mooresville was the town itself, and what I saw as unending opportunities for my children and me. Both of my sons were now old enough to participate in the town's summer programs – swimming lessons, ball teams, day camps, in addition to vacation Bible schools at every church in town.

With Chad's office in the church building, life was different for me. Chad continued to want me to go with him on visits, which I did when not taxiing Dan and Kent around town, but while doing all this, I was secretly filling out an application to Georgia Central College and checking the classified ads in the paper every Sunday for a job.

By autumn of our first year there, I was a student in college studying sociology, and had landed a part-time job in a lawyer's office answering the phone and greeting clients. I managed to schedule my classes in the mornings or early evenings, and worked at the office through the afternoons. The boys came to the office after school and did their homework or entertained themselves quietly in the law library until time to go home at 5:00.

When I had an evening class, they stayed at a friend's house for supper if Chad wasn't able to be home to take care of them. It worked out great for me. The law office was usually quiet in the afternoon, and I could work on my school assignments while listening for the phone to ring. Mr. Belvedere, the lawyer, supported my ambition, and believed that every woman should have an education. I couldn't have found a better place to work. He didn't pay me very much, but it was enough to cover my school supplies and give me a little extra spending money.

I was fortunate to qualify for a Pell Grant and a scholarship, so college tuition wasn't an issue for Chad. And, I didn't have to go to my father for financial help, which pleased me immensely.

Chad claimed in public that he stood behind me one hundred per cent in my endeavors. He often used me as an example in his sermons, and always said encouraging things about my job and schoolwork whenever anyone asked him about it. However, behind closed doors, he'd do his best to knock me down.

"Don't worry about your grades, Fran", he said on more than one occasion. "A *C* is all you need to get by. Don't try to make straight *A*'s. You'll only be disappointed."

And about my job I'd hear, "I wish you didn't feel like you have to work, Fran. I can support the family, you know."

I felt like I was fighting against a strong wind with him, but I was determined to go to school, work, and be a good wife and mother. It was obvious to me that Chad wasn't happy with the way things were going, but he had made a public declaration of his support, so he let me "do my thing", hoping that I'd get discouraged and quit.

I was getting a sample of flying outside of the birdcage. I thrived in school and despite Chad's warnings, made straight *A*'s.

It seemed to irritate him that I did so well, but then he'd rationalize by saying, "Sociology is a crip course of study. It's not as difficult or as deep as Theology."

I pretty much agreed with him, but didn't say so to his face. Sociology was easy for me, and I found it very interesting as I observed the church and how it was a social system in miniature. I made some school friends, and while I wasn't ever included in their lives outside of class, I felt like I was part of a group and not a bird in a birdcage or fish in a fishbowl when I was at the college.

Work, however, was different. Many of Mr. Belvedere's clients were church members, and they were always strangely quiet whenever they came into the office. Chad also found it convenient for keeping an eye on me. Almost every afternoon, he dropped by to say hello and spend a few minutes in the reception area of the office. After a quick check on me, though, he was off somewhere, and I wouldn't see him until he showed up at home for supper.

Because of my job and going to school, I wasn't as involved in church activities as I had been at the previous two churches. I sang in the choir, missing Miss Judith every Sunday I sat in the choir loft. I also attended all of the church dinners, avoiding Mr. Cooper whenever possible. It's odd, though, that I became friendly with Mildred, his wife. While never becoming friends, she always seemed to gravitate toward me at church functions, and we sat next to each other in the choir. She was a beaten-down little lady, always at the beck and call of her husband, but her heart was big, and I always felt that she wished she could speak out to him the way I had at that infamous church supper.

The three years passed quickly. Kent and Dan thrived in school, making good grades and becoming part of the community. They were growing up so fast. When it was time to think about moving again, Dan was in the 6th grade and Kent was in the 4th. It wouldn't be long before they'd be teenagers. I thrived, as well. Not only did we move in June, but I received my Bachelors Degree in Sociology, making all A's, and graduating Summa Cum Laude. Both boys were super proud of their mom.

Chad was miffed.

LEARNING TO SWIM

I go to the *YMCA* two days a week to swim laps. It's a ten-mile drive for me, but it's worth it to get into the pool, lose myself in the rhythm of the strokes, and let my imagination wash over me with the water. I like to go when there aren't many people there, so that I can claim a lane for myself. Sometimes I think I'd like to install a pool here at my house, but I really don't want the responsibility of upkeep or having to vacuum it all spring and summer. Besides, at the *Y* I can swim year-round and let someone else keep the pool clean for me.

I haven't always been a swimmer. As a child I was terrified of the water. If I couldn't touch bottom, I'd panic and grab for the nearest person or post. Chad tried to teach me to swim at the community center where we met. He gave up after I got scared and began to cry after he picked me up and threw me into the deep end of the pool. He apologized profusely — he thought that I'd instinctively swim if I had to. Wrong! I panicked and thrashed my way to the edge of the pool, vowing never to get near it the rest of the summer.

181

As it turned out, when I became a student at Georgia Central College, one of the requirements for graduation was two credit hours of physical education. I tried to get out of it, but no luck. I was stuck. I really didn't have a choice. I knew I didn't want to take basketball or softball - the only other courses offered along with swimming at a time I could take them. I gathered up all of my courage and registered for elementary swimming class.

I was in class with eight other *Terrified Adults*, the title of our swimming class. Our teacher was a woman a little older than me who totally understood how we all felt about the water.

She was a wonder. Before the semester was over, she had us all doing every swimming stroke known to mankind, and as a final exam we had to tread water in the deep end of the pool for five minutes. The magic for me was learning how to relax and let the water hold me up. When I discovered this trick, I was able to do anything. I was very proud of myself - so proud, in fact, I signed up for another semester of swimming lessons in order to complete the physical education requirement.

It was in the second semester that I discovered the joy of swimming laps. All we had to do all semester was show up for class and swim laps for an hour. We counted the laps as we swam, and our grade was determined by the total number we swam during the semester. Of course, I made an *A*.

Along with learning to swim, I also had to face my own modesty about my body. After swimming, we were required to shower, and there were no individual shower stalls in the dressing room. It took every bit of nerve that I had at first to step into the communal shower room and bathe with other women, all of us naked as jaybirds.

At first it was hard for me not to stare, especially at those women who had large breasts. I was so under-endowed, I was fascinated at those huge boobs. After the first week, I trotted into the shower and took my shower without thinking about it. Today, I laugh when I think about those shower episodes, and how the deep end of the swimming pool didn't seem nearly as scary as the shower stall did.

The only part about my going to school that pleased Chad was how swimming firmed up my body. I was fit and slim, and he liked that. More than once during our marriage he warned, "Fran, if you ever get fat, I'll divorce you." I was vain enough to never want to get fat, and I decided that swimming would help me keep my figure.

And so now I still swim. I don't look nearly as good in a bathing suit as I did in my thirties, my breasts aren't as perky as they were then, and my knees are wrinkled. The *Y* I go to has individual showers and dressing areas, but I wouldn't care if I had to shower with other women.

Those two semesters of swimming classes were two of the best courses I took in the three years I was in college.

SEX, RELATIONSHIPS AND PEOPLE

During the time we were in Mooresville, I was so busy working, going to school, talking care of the parsonage and my family, I hardly noticed how Chad was changing.

I was usually so tired at night by the time I went to bed, if he tried to wake me up in the middle of the night for sex, I don't think he could have roused me. But it seemed to me his libido was evening out, and I assumed that it was because he was getting older and wasn't as eager as he was in our early years together. Every now and then, we'd be intimate, or as intimate as a couple can be in the strange positions that he wanted to get into for sex.

He was busier in Broad Street Church than he had been at his previous appointments, and the church was growing, putting more pressure on him to be successful, thus taking his mind off of sex as much as it had been, I thought.

As with the other churches, the women of Broad Street loved Chad, and he gravitated toward them. He always had a group surrounding him whenever there was a church event, and women were always singing his praises to me, telling me how lucky I was to have such a wonderful man for a husband. He loved the women as much as they loved him.

Chad had decided not to play on the church softball team at Broad Street, and he didn't pal around with any of the men of the church or take an active role in the men's groups. He was polite and friendly with the male church members, but I could tell he wasn't comfortable around them as he was with the females.

Paul, the church organist, was a different story. Paul was in his early twenties and a student at Georgia Central, majoring in Music Education. His job at the church helped him pay his bills. A single guy, and very good-looking, he drew lots of women into the church choir. He had a keen wit, and I thoroughly enjoyed choir practice each week, when he'd cut up with the choir director, Ann Nelson, and make the evening one of both work and fun. He was already entrenched in the church when we arrived, and Chad liked him at once.

Paul even talked Chad into taking piano lessons from him, which surprised me, since Chad was absolutely tone deaf. Paul assured me that he could teach Chad to read music and at the very least play some simple tunes on the piano. Both of them were up for the challenge.

They met at the church every Tuesday afternoon after Paul's classes at college and worked together for an hour or so. I never saw or heard Chad practice, since we didn't have a piano in the parsonage, and he wasn't eager to show off for me what he'd learned. It seemed to make Chad happy, and Paul didn't charge him a fee – we paid him with dinner at the parsonage on Tuesday evenings – so there was nothing for me to object to.

Other than Paul, Chad didn't have any male friends as far as I knew, except for his buddy, Joe. I didn't hear much about Joe anymore. I assumed he had moved up in the church world and had outgrown Chad.

I was glad that they liked each other. I felt like Chad needed a good male friend. Chad's piano lessons only lasted a few months. I suspected that Paul found his musically-challenged minister to be too difficult to teach, and soon Chad lost interest after not being able to experience success at the keyboard.

Paul resigned the church position not long after the lessons ended. He transferred to Georgia State University and moved to Atlanta, where he secured a job as organist and choir director of a large city church. It was a big step up for him, although we missed him at Broad Street.

There were times when a fleeting thought would cross my mind that Chad might be interested in someone else. I hadn't gotten to the point of thinking that he could have an affair, but he was so cozy with the women in the church, I had to admit that from time to time the thought crossed my mind that he might be seeing someone behind my back. He seldom talked to me about his afternoon visitations, or told me where he had gone or who he had visited. One day when I asked him where he'd been, he took on his famous victim's expression, and accused me of not trusting him.

"I trust you, Chad," I said. "I was only curious about where you were this afternoon." And in my usual fashion, I ended up apologizing to him profusely and asking his forgiveness for even posing the question.

He took me in his arms, hugging me, and said, "Of course I forgive you, Fran. You mean the world to me. Now, let's just drop it."

Which I did. I never did find out who he had visited that afternoon or where he had been.

On the other hand, Chad questioned me about everything – where I went, who I talked to, what I was doing. During the time I was at work at the law office, he could stop by anytime to see me. However, when I was in school, he grew jealous of my time. He did everything in his power to get me to quit college. When his little verbal jabs about my potential failure didn't work with me, he took on the tack of it being an affront to him as my provider.

"Your place is at home, Fran, where you can be a good minister's wife," was one avenue he took.

"I'm the breadwinner of the family We should be following the Bible's instruction on the woman's place in the home," was another.

"The boys need for you to be home in case they get sick," was his way of getting our sons into the picture.

And then, he'd get the church members involved, "What are our church members going to think if you aren't available to do your share in the church?"

As a last resort, he attacked my housekeeping habits, accusing me of abusing my responsibility as a minister's wife to keep the parsonage clean and tidy at all times. Our home was far from picture-book perfect, but I never knew Chad to lift a finger to help around the house. Whenever I'd ask him to help, he'd come back with, "I have more important things to do. Fran, this is your job."

I listened to his every argument, and always returned with, "Chad, I am going to get my degree. I don't want to be out in the cold without a way to make a living if something should happen to you. Besides, the house won't cave in if it doesn't get vacuumed every day."

"Nothing's going to happen to me. You don't have anything to worry about," was his standard reply, but it wasn't enough to make me change the course for my future.

I also didn't think our church members cared one bit what I did or didn't do. Most of the women in our congregation had jobs, and I didn't think any of them thought any less of either Chad or me if I continued going to school. The only time any members came to our house was for the annual Christmas Open House. I made sure the house was spotless, at least once a year.

In many ways I was a mouse when it came to Chad and what he wanted from me, but on this matter - getting a degree - I was determined, and I was gradually becoming stronger from the inside out, even if I was not yet at the point of wanting to exert myself against him.

A MYSTERY IN THE CHURCH WORLD

I was very busy, going to school, learning to swim, working in the law office, being a mom and attempting to be a good preacher's wife. I didn't have time to keep up with the goings-on of other ministers' families, but I got wind of something one day that shook me to the core.

I happened to run into the minister's wife of a small church on the outskirts of town one afternoon while grocery shopping. We stopped to chat and catch up on what each other was doing, and how our kids were getting along in school.

She said, "Have you heard the big news about Joe and Lori Carter? Aren't you and Chad good friends with them?"

"What news?" I asked, expecting to learn something about a big promotion or recognition for Joe.

"They're gone. Nobody seems to know where they are," she answered.

I was astounded. "What do you mean – *gone?*"

"Well, the talk is that something really bad happened at their church. I've heard that he got caught having an affair with his secretary, that Lori caught him with another church member, and that he embezzled money from the church. Who knows what the true story is. I was hoping that maybe you knew."

"I haven't heard a thing," I answered, as I tried to grasp what I was hearing. "I haven't talked to Lori in a long time," I confessed.

"Well, if you find out, will you let me know? I'm dying to know what the real story is."

I assured her I would, but knew I probably wouldn't. This was the kind of gossip that could do a lot of damage, and I didn't want to be part of it.

That night, at home, I asked Chad if he knew anything about it. He didn't seem surprised, but only shrugged and said, "Fran, it's none of our business. Best to just leave it alone."

"But you and Joe are such good friends," I started, only to be stopped in my tracks.

"*Leave it alone, Fran.* And don't go adding your two-cents worth to the local gossip." He was done talking. I knew I'd never get anything out of him, even if he knew. And I was sure he knew a lot more than I did.

The next day, I tried to get in touch with Lori, but their phone number had been changed, and no forwarding number was available. I then tried writing, but my letter was returned to me with no forwarding address.

They had all disappeared – into thin air, it seemed.

I was baffled.

GOD VERSUS FRAN – ROUND 200

A few months ago, a former church member found me through Facebook on the Internet. Caught totally by surprise, I was astounded at her message to me.

"Fran, you'll never know how much you meant to me when you and Chad were at Broad Street. Your kind and loving support pulled me through one of the worst periods of my life. I am so happy to have found you again. I hope you are doing well and are happy at last."

I didn't have a clue that I had meant anything to those people. After I moved out of parsonages forever, it felt like the church doors had been slammed in my face. I never heard from anyone again, except for a few letters from Chad's fan club who wrote to tell me what a horrible person I was for abandoning such a wonderful man. Maybe I made a larger impact on people than I ever thought, since nobody ever told me. All I heard all those years was how wonderful Chad was!

It took me many years to forgive the church, forgive Chad, and forgive all those fine Christian people. But I did, and from where I sit now, I can look at the picture in its entirety. And, after receiving this kind message, I can see that in some strange way I was in a place where I was supposed to be, even though I didn't understand it at the time and I felt very lonely and isolated much of the time. Perhaps that is where God wanted me to be in order to teach me how to be the person I am today.

I don't argue with God the way I did during those parsonage days. However, I continue to question him and religion in general as I seek my own path through the universe. I have come to a sense of peace that Christianity for me isn't quite what Chad preached and the church taught, but I wage no more battles with the Southern Evangelical Church. I still do not pray aloud in public, and hesitate to even ask a blessing at a meal. I am also known to cringe at things I hear coming from the pulpit of Wellspring Methodist Church, but it passes like a shiver and I move on without passing judgment on what I consider narrow-minded religion.

I do question at times what people claim to be God's calling into the ministry. From my personal experience, I have known a few ministers who I believe were truly divinely called, singled out by God for this particular profession, and who were somehow different from the rest of us, in a spiritual sense. The rest I've encountered over the years seem to me to be people who are in the ministry for a variety of reasons, claiming what they believe is God's calling as their reason and rationale for being where they are and for doing what they believe is a special directive from heaven. Then there are those who use ministry and the church as a form of escape or a good place to atone for some deep-seeded guilt or for something else lacking in their lives.

I don't see what is labeled a call into ministry as being more special than a person being inspired to become a doctor, a teacher, a police officer, an accountant - or any vocation, for that matter - that one feels led or motivated to pursue. I also finally came to the understanding that perhaps God wanted me to do something special with my life, something that didn't have anything to do with Chad's profession. He just chose a strange way of showing me.

In Chad's case, I am convinced that his calling into ministry was a form of escape, a justification for his guilt, and a way for him to live that required little effort on his part. He liked having the church take care of him, provide him with a home and a paycheck, and be a place where he could hide, and not have to face the real world. It was what my dad called "the path of least resistance." He was a natural actor and entertainer, and preaching fit the bill for him while making him feel like he was doing God's will and somehow atoning for things in his life that weren't so noble.

But then, that's just my opinion.

A SUNDAY BLOW-UP

One Sunday after church, Chad and I were sitting in the living room of the parsonage watching a football game on TV. The boys were outside playing, so it was just the two of us in the house. In an attempt to have a conversation with him, I mentioned how much I had enjoyed the Sunday School class I had taught that morning to one of the ladies' classes.

"So, what did you tell the ladies about me?" he asked.

"Nothing," I replied. "The lesson was on God's forgiveness and redemption. It had nothing to do about you. It was an Old Testament lesson."

"I know that you talk to those women about me, and put me down in front of them," he accused.

"No, I don't!" I exclaimed, my voice rising to a higher pitch. "I never say anything about you or us to anyone in the church!"

"Don't lie to me, Fran. I know that you're going around behind my back talking about me."

"I am not lying," my voice increasing in volume. "Why would you accuse me of such a thing?"

With that, I ran to the bedroom and shut the door behind me. I was crying and felt like I'd been stabbed in the heart. I thought he'd follow me into the bedroom like he usually did whenever we had a spat, but this time all I heard was the sound of his car backing out of the driveway.

I pulled myself together and when the boys came inside and asked me where their dad had gone, I told them that he was called out on a church emergency. I didn't want them to know what had happened, but I'm sure the signs of my tears gave me away with them. They could tell that I was distressed, and I hoped that they thought that whatever called their father away was what was upsetting to me.

I spent the rest of the afternoon wondering where Chad was. I tried to occupy myself with reading a book I had put off beginning, but I couldn't concentrate. This paranoia was getting worse with him, and I didn't understand why he mistrusted me the way he did.

By late afternoon, I wasn't as angry as I was earlier. Now I was getting worried. I kept going to the living room window to see if I could spot him driving down our road. What if he had been in an accident? He was mad when he left, and he might have taken out his anger on the car. Where could he be? I knew he wouldn't leave for good, but I really didn't know where he could be. I didn't dare call anyone to ask if they'd seen him – that would only lead to questions that I couldn't answer. I finally went into the kitchen and warmed up some leftovers for the boys and me to have for supper.

As we were finishing our meal, which I could hardly eat, in walked Chad, smiling as if nothing had happened. I held my tongue until after Dan and Kent left the table to go upstairs to finish their homework to ask him about it.

"You scared me to death," I said. "I didn't know where you were, or if something terrible might have happened to you. Where did you go, anyway?"

"I just needed to drive around for a little while," was his offhand answer. "And then I stopped at the mall theater to see a movie. There was no need for you to worry."

"Well, I *was* worried, and I *was* upset. Are you sure you're OK?"

"I'm fine, Fran. I was just needed some time to be alone," was his terse answer.

I decided to try to bring us back to companionship. "What movie did you see?" I asked.

I could see the mask cover his face telling me that this was none of my business. "I don't even remember what it was. I was in a fog, and sat in the theater the whole time not paying a bit of attention to the movie."

I instinctively knew not to pursue this line of questioning and to let it drop. Chad didn't want to talk to me about the afternoon, and I didn't want to put up a wall between us any higher than the one we were gradually building. He quickly changed clothes and left to go to the church's evening activities. The boys and I stayed home. I didn't have to make up an excuse of having a headache. Mine was genuine.

That night, Chad awakened me around 2:00 am, and we had what I considered frantic sex. If I had put a timer to it, I don't think it lasted over five minutes from start to finish. In one way, I felt relieved that he wanted to have sex with me, but in another way, it stirred up a whole bunch of unanswered questions. In many ways, I was still that meek little mouse who only wanted to have a happy home, a family, and a sense of security.

I didn't want to muddy the waters around me.

SECOND VERSE, SAME AS THE FIRST

More moves, and finally with each one a slight move up. Money problems eased somewhat as Chad made higher salaries, even though he continued to keep us on a strict cash-only budget. He still didn't like the idea of my having a job of my own, and when I worked, my income went into the family account, and my allotment for my monthly expenses didn't go up accordingly. Whenever I'd confront Chad about needing more cash, he'd only laugh at me and tell me to manage my money better.

During the next few years, I only worked sporadically, mainly because Chad wasn't happy when I worked, and I wanted to keep peace in the house. Chad was getting harder and harder to figure out. He wanted me to be an active participant in his ministry, yet his suspicions over who I might be talking to was always an issue. I walked a tightrope trying to be a good minister's wife while keeping him satisfied that I wasn't telling secrets about him to the people I came in contact with. I couldn't imagine what he thought I might be saying.

Both boys were very active in school activities, so it made it easier if I didn't hold down a full-time job and was available to serve as carpool driver and spectator for whatever activity they were involved in at the time. I had earned my degree and felt more comfortable about my ability to take care of myself should the need arise. Life was far from perfect, but I had accomplished my goal.

The boys were growing up. When we left Broad Street, Dan was 12 and Kent was 10. They were still sweet kids, but I saw with the move from Broad Street to Westview Church in the suburbs of Atlanta that future moves were going to become more and more difficult for them as they reached high school age.

They both did well in school, even with frequent upheavals in their lives, and I was very proud of them and their accomplishments. Dan seemed headed in the direction of leadership as he joined the school debate team and participated in school government. Kent was an entertainer like his dad, and everywhere he went, he made friends right off the bat. He loved music and sang in the school choral group, as well as participated in the theater program. Both boys enjoyed sports and were good tennis players and strong swimmers, but neither of them opted to participate in the school sports programs.

It concerned me that Dan and Kent began making excuses not to go to church. They didn't like being sermon topics, hearing their dad embellish stories about them to make a point to the congregation. They also felt singled out as "P.K.'s", and as adolescents felt different from their friends. While Chad always loved telling family stories as part of his sermons, he agreed not to use the boys as examples from the pulpit any more. We also agreed that they could attend youth activities at other churches, just as long as they went with a friend. This arrangement lasted about a year – they were both soon back in our church with a new appreciation of their own church, even if their dad was the minister. They realized that they were preacher's kids, no matter what church they attended, and they put up with it on their home turf until they left for college.

I had an uneasy feeling all of the time that something was going to happen where I'd need my education, but I pushed it back every time it reared its ugly head from the recesses of my mind.

After Chad's buddy, Joe, left the ministry, two other ministers that we knew did the same. These weren't as mysterious as the Joe and Lori disappearances, though. The first one was caught having an affair with a church member. His wife divorced him with record speed, and he was moved to a church across the state, a much larger church in a good-sized city. I heard that he married the woman he was involved with, and I always wondered how he pulled that one off. One of my minister's wives' friends dubbed it a "flop to the top."

The second one was health-related. He had a stroke and could no longer serve the church. He and his family were shoved out of their parsonage as soon as he recovered enough to move. The last I heard was that he was selling insurance. I didn't know any of the details, but I was beginning to think that the church could certainly play favorites as well as be very unfeeling to her ministers.

COUNTING THE DOLLARS

All these years later, there is one habit from my marriage that has stayed with me. I continue to add up how much I am spending when I go to the grocery store.

One day not too long ago when Dan and Kent were visiting me, we went together to the grocery store to pick up some things we needed. I had my pad and pencil with me, and I was marking the price of each item we put into the basket, keeping a running total of what I was spending.

When the boys were growing up, we did the same thing. As soon as we reached the total of the amount of money I had in my purse, our shopping was done. Sometimes, we'd have to backtrack to put something back on the shelf so that we'd have the money for an item we really needed. And, if we finished our shopping and hadn't reached our total, the boys could select a treat and put it into the cart. With the strict budget Chad kept me on, this was the only way I had of keeping track and not embarrassing myself at check-out.

On this particular day, Dan was walking beside me while Kent was ahead of us, scoping out the store.

Dan said, "You know, Mom, of all the things I learned from you, this is the thing that has paid off the most. You taught me how to make the best use of whatever money I have and how to keep a budget."

I was astounded. "I always thought that I was depriving you boys of things you wanted to have. I never dreamed that it was a good thing."

We continued down the aisle when Dan added, "Dad was always trying to keep you under his thumb, wasn't he? I'm really proud of you, Mom."

I couldn't say anything more than a choked-up "Thank you." And thankfully, about that time Kent came rushing up behind us in the aisle, trying to scare us. He and Dan got into a mock scuffle, pushing and shoving each other playfully. You'd think they were 12 and 10 again!

"OK, boys, you keep acting like this and I'll never take you to the store again," I teased.

To which Kent countered, "Mom, remember the time you took us to the store and we were acting so bad? You told us then that you'd never take us back into a grocery store until we were both over 35. Well, we're older than that now. You're stone cold out of luck!"

We all laughed and continued our shopping. I put the pad and pencil away and took my chances at the cash register.

FAMILY DYNAMICS

Chad was never close to his parents. When we got married, it felt as if his father dusted his hands of all parental authority and sent Chad off on his own. Mr. Sammons, an accountant, had worked his way up in a major corporation, motivated by money and prestige. Chad's mother, a sweet and petite little lady, adored her husband, and whatever he did was fine with her. She went along with whatever he decided. We hardly ever heard from them, even though they lived no more than a few hours' drive from us regardless of where we were.

After Chad announced to them that he was going to become a preacher, Chad's father never quite understood what his son was doing. Mr. Sammons thought his son was making a huge mistake going into the ministry, but then he wasn't happy when Chad was a coach and teacher. There didn't seem to be much that Chad could do to make his father proud of him.

Mom was proud of her son, regardless, but she had to be very quiet in praising him or giving him any kind of support. She didn't dare cross her husband. Chad didn't talk about his folks much, and neither of us talked to them on the phone, except on special occasions. I sensed that there was something much deeper than what appeared on the surface between Chad and his father, but as was typical of me, I didn't probe. His dad didn't seem to have any affection for me, so it wasn't a big issue, as far as I was concerned. I often thought about his mom, though, and wished that I could somehow get closer to her. Maybe she could have given me some insight on her son.

They didn't have much to do with their grandchildren, either. I always felt that Chad's mom wanted to see our boys, but whenever we'd invite them to our home or suggest that we go visit them, his dad would find a reason not to get together. The boys always received a birthday card from her every year with a $20 bill in it, as well as a nice gift for Christmas - always mailed, never delivered.

My parents, on the other hand, missed us like crazy, and always made sure to make at least one trip to visit us each year. And, after my famous trip to see them the time Chad got so upset with me, I made a point of going down to Florida with the boys every summer to spend a few days with their grandparents. If Chad wasn't busy, he'd go with us, but like his dad, he could almost always find an excuse not to accompany us on these trips.

Chad liked to call me "Daddy's Little Girl" and accused me of loving my father more than I loved him. In many ways, he was correct. I could always count on getting support and love from my dad, while as time went on, the only thing I could rely on from Chad was a put-down or accusation. I sometimes felt it odd that Chad didn't disapprove of these trips, when he always wanted me close by otherwise. Perhaps he had developed enough trust in me to believe that I wouldn't get into any trouble at my parents' home.

By the time Chad had moved up in the ministry enough to possibly make his father proud – being a minister of a fairly large church with a very nice parsonage, both of his parents had died. His mother died of a heart attack at age 60, and his father of lung cancer a couple of years later. He refused any kind of therapy, accusing the doctors of wanting to poison him for his money.

I attended his mother's funeral, but Chad didn't want me or the boys to go to his dad's. Since Chad was an only child, both services were small. I was surprised that there wasn't much of an inheritance for Chad, but I really didn't care. After all of the medical bills were paid and the house was sold, we received a check for $50,000. Chad didn't want any of his parents' furniture or belongings, and hired a moving company to haul everything to the Salvation Army. Chad socked the money away into the boys' college funds, and that was it. It was as if he finished reading a book and put it away on a top shelf, never to look at it or open it up again.

MEMORIES GET JUMBLED UP AS THE END NEARED

After leaving Broad Street Church, I followed Chad to three more churches and parsonages. I had fallen into the ebb and flow of the life of the minister's wife.

With each move there were similarities, and with each move there were new adventures. I became more and more numb emotionally with each new place, going through the motions of what was required of me, and protecting myself from feeling much of anything.

The parsonages were becoming strangely similar, and the Parsonage Committees were all the same, as well. I used my skills at manipulation to get what I wanted in each parsonage, and became very good at it.

By the time the boys were both in high school, I had become adjusted to fishbowl and birdcage life. I was used to being on display in the church as Chad's adoring and pretty wife, and swam around my fishbowl home without complaining.

I began to think that my looks were all that Chad cared about – he noticed if I ever gained a pound or two, and urged me to color the gray hairs that were beginning to give me a salt and pepper look. I had also grown accustomed to his obsession over what he thought I was saying about him, and assured him over and again that as a minister's wife, there was no way I could confide in church members, and I certainly wouldn't tell anyone our personal business.

I longed for a place of my own, but I knew this wasn't in the cards for me as long as I was with Chad. And I wasn't brave enough to even think about an alternative. Every now and again, I'd fantasize that something would happen to Chad, forcing me to move out of the parsonage and have a life of my own, but then I'd suffer a huge sense of guilt over such thoughts and push them aside. My prayers to God often centered around asking forgiveness for such thoughts.

I began scrutinizing my feelings for Chad. I didn't give much thought whether I loved him or not, but when I looked back to the way I felt during our early years together, I admitted to myself that things had certainly changed. Chad was right when he complained that I didn't need or love him as much as he did me, at least not anymore.

While I was living in the shadows of the church and of Chad, I was gaining strength as an individual in my own right. I still didn't make waves, but went through the motions of what was expected of me. I didn't think about whether I loved him, and I didn't hide behind him anymore. I didn't need to. I was the Invisible Woman.

I played the role of referee when moving time came, as the boys were growing less and less enthusiastic about going to a new community and school, but somehow I was successful in making each move a positive event for my sons. Chad didn't change his ways when looking for a new church to serve, and I found myself quietly and subversively exerting my influence behind the scenes on behalf of my sons as far as where their future home would be. I didn't particularly like the person I turned into during these periods, but rationalized it all as a survival mechanism. I told myself I was simply being a mother and protecting my children before considering my husband.

When Dan got his driver's license, I truly felt like a bird let out of a cage. No longer were my days bound by carpool schedules. Chad bought him an old used car, which delighted us all. Dan now drove himself and his brother to school every day, and also to school activities.

I got a part-time job in a small insurance agency, which gave me some independence and also an excuse to get out of the parsonage. This time Chad didn't object to my working, and I could literally feel the pall of the preacher's wife life start to lift from my shoulders during those times when he was out of pocket. Chad continued to check in on me when I was at work, but then he would disappear for hours without letting me know where he was. I assumed that he was making hospital and nursing home visits to members of his flock, while in the back of my mind the thought that perhaps he was involved in some extra-curricular activity became a more frequent visitor.

By the time we moved into our sixth parsonage, both boys were now in college and living in campus apartments. I didn't care anymore about where we lived or what our home was like. I was tired of Chad's strange habits and weird ways in our private life. It was as if he were a totally different person when he walked through the church doors than the one he was in the parsonage.

Now that Dan and Kent were gone from the house except for school holidays, Chad and I settled into more of a roommate way of life than that of a married couple. Sex became at most a weekly activity, and I felt as if Chad was making love to me simply because it was something he was supposed to do.

He grew more and more distant and secretive with me. My fantasies of something happening to him came in greater frequency, and the vision of my future was getting fuzzier and fuzzier. I knew instinctively that something was about to happen

PART THREE

DISCOVERIES

Jennie Campbell

A STRANGE WEDDING

It was a Saturday morning in September. Both boys had gone back to their respective colleges. I was in the bedroom getting dressed for my day off from work, and had plans for how I would spend the day. It was a typical Saturday, including grocery shopping, doing laundry, going for a long walk – all of the things a working woman does on her day off.

Chad entered the bedroom, demanding to know what I was doing. When I laid out my plans to him, he said "Fran, you'll have to change them. I have a wedding this afternoon, and I want you to go with me."

"Who's getting married?" I asked, wracking my brain to remember who in the church had wedding plans.

"It's going to be a garden wedding, and then the reception," Chad said. "You don't know them. They aren't church members."

"Well, then, I don't think I'll go," I answered. "You can take care of this by yourself."

"Fran, you are going with me. I told them that you'd be there."

"Chad, I said I don't want to go. I don't know these people, and I don't need to go," I countered.

"Fran," he said in a low and threatening voice. "Either you go with me, or you can get out. If you can't act like a preacher's wife, then maybe you'd better think about leaving."

I couldn't believe what I was hearing. "And where would I go?"

"You can always go home. Your daddy would love to have his little girl back," was his answer.

I looked at Chad with a look of total disbelief. "Are you trying to get rid of me? Why are you saying this?"

It was like a cloud suddenly lifted from his face, replacing his anger with a stricken expression. He moved toward me, his arms extended. I stood like a statue and let him embrace me.

"Oh, Fran," he whispered. "I didn't mean that. I've been under such pressure lately, I don't know what I was thinking. Of course I don't want you to leave me. What would I do without you? Please go to this wedding with me. I am so sorry."

Dumbfounded, I mumbled something back to him assuring him that I'd go to the wedding and reception.

It was a strained afternoon. I stood along the fringes of the garden where the wedding was held, not speaking to anybody. As I listened to Chad performing the ceremony, I thought back to our wedding and all of the dreams I had of my picture book marriage. It certainly hadn't turned out the way I had envisioned that day so many years ago. After all of the vows were said, and the newly married couple was introduced to the wedding guests, everyone moved as one into the large antebellum home where the reception was to be held.

I waited for Chad. He was the last one to exit the garden, and had taken off his clerical robe, draping it over his arm. He asked me to wait where I was while he put it into the car. By the time we entered the hall, a live band was playing and the bride and groom were dancing the traditional wedding dance. We found a cocktail table where nobody was sitting and sat down to watch the festivities.

We had barely settled ourselves when a waiter with a tray of wine glasses approached us asking if we preferred red or white.

I was on the verge of saying "No, thank you," when Chad requested two glasses of white. What was this? In all the years he had been a minister, we'd never had any alcoholic beverages, either in our home or in public. Chad handed me one of the glasses, winked at me, and with the clink of his glass on mine, he said, "To us." I took a sip and placed my goblet on the table.

"Would you like to dance?" he asked as he finished the last drop of his wine.

"No, I don't think so," I answered, to which he took me by the arm and forcibly led me onto the dance floor. He drew me close to him, and sang into my ear with his off-key voice along with The Carpenter's famous song, *We've Only Just Begun.*

When we returned to our table, he looked at me with an expression I could only describe as a half-sneer, "See, Fran, aren't you glad you came with me?"

"Yes, I am" I lied.

FRAN, THE PRIVATE INVESTIGATOR

As I think about the day when Chad gave me my ultimatum, I consider it the beginning of the end. He scared me that day, and something inside of me bolted into action. I began looking back over our marriage and questioning things I had never questioned, and examining things I had been too meek to investigate.

Things were getting too bizarre for me to brush off as normal, and my rationalization of having little experience with men except for Chad didn't hold water any longer. It's easy now for me to see the mural of our life together, and point straight to the warning signs, but at the time it was like unfolding a treasure map, a treasure I didn't want to find.

I began by paying more attention to what Chad was doing and where he went. It occurred to me that he was making far too many hospital and funeral home visits. When I checked the church bulletin each week in the section entitled *Parish Needs*, most weeks there weren't enough sick people or dead people to fill up the amount of time he was spending away from the church and parsonage.

I began looking for signs of an affair – the scent of perfume on his clothes, strands of hair in his car or on his jackets, all of the things I'd seen on television detective programs. As with every church he served, the women of the church adored him, but I began to see that while he loved the attention he got from them, he didn't pay any one woman more attention than another. To him, they were his groupies, bolstering his ego and making him feel important. He was their rock star, and the entertainer in him loved the attention.

So, if Chad wasn't having an affair, what could he be doing? I ruled out drugs, even though he had smoked a little pot back in our early days together. He was making a pretty decent salary now, but I didn't think he had enough in his budget to afford illegal drugs. At the time I didn't consider that he might be selling drugs, or I might have investigated the possibility. As it turned out, it wasn't drugs at all.

As I reflected more and more, and dug back deeper and deeper into our past, I thought about Joe. I hadn't heard anything about him since we were at Broad Street when I heard that he had left the ministry. He and Chad had been very close buddies. I was convinced that Chad had kept up with him, but we never spoke about it. I bet he could help me. I didn't have a clue where he was, but I was sure that Chad knew.

I couldn't ask Chad, so I went to the public library and began searching through the state criss-cross directories. I hit pay dirt. Not only did I find an address and telephone number for Joe in Atlanta, but I found a listing for L. R. Carter in a small town in south Georgia. Somewhere in our friendship, Lori had told me that her maiden name was Redding, and this popped into my mind. I made a note of it, and planned to send a note to find out if this might be Lori. If I called her on the phone, it would have to be from the office where I worked, since Chad paid all of our bills, and would see the long distance charge. I wasn't sure who to contact first, but decided to try Joe, since it would be a local call.

I worked up my courage one evening while Chad was out visiting new church members. I didn't know what I was going to say if Joe actually answered the phone, but I figured that it would come to me.

Surprised that he answered on the second ring, I stammered out who I was, and asked if this was the Joe Carter who had once been a minister.

His voice sounded puzzled. "Fran, is that you? Is something wrong with Chad?" he asked.

I was quick to assure him, "Joe, Chad is fine. What I'm calling about is that I'm hoping that maybe you can help me with something."

"What is it, Fran? You know I'll be glad to help in any way I can. Are you guys in trouble of some kind?"

"I'm not sure, Joe. Chad has been acting very strange lately, and knowing that you two are such good friends, I was hoping that you might know if there is something going on that I should know about." I was really reaching, and realized that Joe might not want to violate a confidence.

It was at that moment that I heard another man's voice in the background. "Hey Joe, I'm here. What's happenin'?" The voice sounded familiar. It was Chad's.

Into the phone Joe said to me in a hushed voice, "Fran, this isn't a good time to talk. I'll call you back later." He hung up.

It hit me like the combination between a slap in the face and a bucket of cold water. There wasn't another woman.

And Joe never called me back.

WHAT TO DO NOW?

I was never so relieved that both our sons were away at college. While my whole life crumbled at my feet, I held the phone receiver to my heart, stunned. As I came to my senses, realizing what I had just heard - and assumed - my brain was going 100 miles an hour. Maybe I was wrong. It could have been a coincidence that Chad was visiting Joe at the same time I made the phone call. Everything in me was fighting with what I instinctively knew. I had to find out for sure.

Screw Chad and his budget! I was going to phone Lori. I dialed the number I had written down for L.R. Carter, my hands shaking. I sat down, waiting for the voice on the other end to answer. When it did, I recognized Lori's voice immediately.

"Lori?" I hesitantly asked.

"Yes, this is Lori."

"Lori, this is Fran. I need to talk to you."

There was a silence from the other end of the line.

Then, "I was hoping you wouldn't find me, Fran. But I knew you would, eventually. You know, don't you?"

"Then it's true?" I asked. "It's Chad and Joe?"

"Yes, it was. How did you find out?" she asked.

"Lori, I think it's not *was* but *still is*", I answered. "Why didn't you tell me?"

"Fran, it was a long time ago. Both guys were moving up in their ministries. Joe got caught, but wanted to protect Chad. He thought Chad was one of the best young ministers in the whole conference. I promised to keep quiet in exchange for letting me and the girls exit the scene quietly. I also believed that it was Chad's job to tell you, not mine. I'm so sorry."

Before I had time to respond, she asked, "Fran, what are you going to do?"

"I have a lot to think about, Lori," I sighed. "Chad hasn't said anything to me yet. I'm not even sure if he knows that I know. I don't know what to do."

Again, "Fran, I am so sorry. I wish this didn't have to happen, but I guess I knew in my heart that this day would come for you. I got away and started a new life with my girls. Maybe you can do the same. If you ever need me, I'm here."

"Thanks, Lori. I just feel numb right now. I've thought that Chad might be having an affair for a long time, but it never crossed my mind that he might be gay. It's too much for me to believe right now," I answered. "I don't know what is going to happen."

After a brief conversation in an attempt to sound normal, we caught each other up on our kids and what they were doing. When I hung up, I collapsed onto the floor, drew my body up as tight as I could, and sobbed.

Thankfully, it was a couple of hours before Chad came home. I had pulled myself together, taken a hot shower and attempted to erase the signs of my teary outburst. I had to be calm. I had to be smart. I didn't know if Joe had told Chad about my phone call. I had to be ready for anything.

From the sounds of Chad's entering the house and walking toward the kitchen to grab a snack, I could tell that Joe hadn't said anything to him. Nothing seemed out of the ordinary.

"Fran," he called out. "I'm home. Where are you?"

"In the bedroom," I called back. "I just got out of the shower."

I tried to walk as nonchalantly as possible down the hall, wrapping the tie of my robe around my waist. Entering the kitchen, I sat down on one of the bar stools and said to my husband, while intently focusing on his face, "You'll never guess who I talked to on the phone tonight." I paused for effect. "Lori Carter."

"Really?" was his brief response, but I could see a shadow of panic cross his face. "Did she call you?"

"No, I called her. There was something I had to find out from her."

He knew that I knew. Visibly shaken, he sat down at the bar across from me, never letting his gaze leave my face. "What did you find out?"

"Chad, you know," was all I said.

I won't go into detail the next few hours. In a nutshell, Chad cried, pleaded, cajoled, confessed, begged for forgiveness, and implored me not to say anything to anyone.

I surprised myself at my strength. All those years I had been walking on eggshells around him, sup- porting him even when I didn't understand why, and catering to his strange ways in my effort to keep peace in our home – all of this flew out the parsonage windows that night. I didn't want to know details of the past twenty years – I only wanted to figure out what to do next. All of the reminiscing and analyzing could come later.

"Fran, please don't tell anyone about this. I can't lose my job or my position in the church conference. I don't know what I'll do if you leave me. I need you. I can't lose you," he begged.

There was something inside of me that felt very sorry for Chad. He had lived this secret for years, probably even since before we got married. I was the only person in his life who had believed in him and supported him in his ministry. And now it was within my power to ruin him.

I thought back to all the years of moving from one parsonage to another, from one church to another, following Chad because I believed that he was called by God to be a minister. I remembered all of the First Sundays, parsonage open houses, soiled mattresses and crummy furniture, church jobs I didn't want, and feelings of guilt over not being happy doing God's will. My sympathy turned to anger and bitterness as he begged and pleaded.

I searched for words to say to him, but none were there.

"Chad, I need some time to think," I finally said. "I won't stay with you, continue to live a lie, and put up with this shit any longer," I finally said, using a curse word that I seldom uttered. "And I have to think about Dan and Kent, too. I'll sleep in Dan's room tonight."

As I nestled down into my older son's bed that night, and waited for sleep that never came, my whole life played before my eyes.

Thinking about Chad cheating on me, especially with another man, made me nauseous and with wave after wave of realization hitting me, I thought I was going to vomit. I wished it had been a woman – and thought possibly that might be the case, as well. All of the strange sexual aspects of our marriage filled my mind, and I was truly befuddled. It was enough for me to know that my husband was unfaithful, but adding the homosexual dimension to it was more than I could handle that night.

It was in my power to ruin him, end his career, and make myself a martyr. And I didn't know what to tell our sons. They were both grown men now, but I didn't want to be the one to tell them about their dad. Was this a secret I could keep? Was it one that I *should* keep? I thought about Chad in the other bedroom. I was sure that he was having a sleepless night, as well, but on that night I was being very self-centered and thinking only about myself and why this had to happen to me.

Toward sunrise, my decision was made and I began working on a plan. I determined to keep Chad's secret. It was his life, and his responsibility to either live with the secret or come out and admit who he was.

I decided to move out of the parsonage – I'd make up an excuse for going to another town, perhaps a professional opportunity I couldn't resist. My first priority was to find a job. I would become the bad guy in this scenario, thus preserving Chad's reputation with the church and with his congregation. As far as Dan and Kent were concerned, I'd tell them that now that they were grown, I needed to finally fulfill my dream of having a career. I was not going to be the one to tell them that their father was gay, or possibly bisexual, at least not now.

There was no rush as far as I could tell. If possible, I would make my move before conference time in June. I had become very skilled over the years in hiding my feelings and putting on a mask to be someone I wasn't. This would be no different. I knew I could do it. Whatever Chad decided to do was his business.

It wasn't that I was being noble or high-and-mighty in taking this track. I was completely shattered, thinking that my husband had led a double life all these years, and that I was too naïve and trusting until recently to suspect anything. It had not occurred to me that he was a gay man. I didn't know much about homosexuality except for the flamboyant characters I had seen sashaying up and down a beach boardwalk one summer while on vacation. And I had suspected that Paul, the organist at Broad Street Church, was gay, but never thought much about it; he was such a nice guy and I liked him very much. His sexual orientation was never an issue with me. I now entertained the thought that perhaps he and Chad… I refused to follow this line of thought any further.

I was also boiling inside recognizing the coward I had been in our marriage in my attempt to please my husband and to stand beside him in his calling. I wasn't sure now about his call into the ministry as one from God, but I was certain that his profession was one that he was dedicated to and one in which he excelled. He'd be lost without his pulpit and his church.

The next few weeks were very difficult, to say the least. I could hardly look at Chad without my blood boiling and my eyes tearing up. I asked Chad to concoct a professional development trip to get him out of the house for a few days so that I could talk to the boys. Knowing that I now had the upper hand, he cooperated with my wishes. He left on a Friday afternoon, saying that he was attending a ministers' retreat. He arranged for a substitute preacher to fill in for him on Sunday.

I asked Dan and Kent if they would come home that week-end to stay with me. It was going to be awfully hard lying to them, but I justified to myself that I wouldn't really be telling them a lie, I would merely leave out a few facts. They were both curious about why I wanted them both to come home, but agreed to spend the weekend with me and didn't ask any probing questions, for which I was thankful.

When I told them of my plans to go back to work full-time, hopefully doing something related to my college degree, they were supportive and told me it sounded like a good idea. They asked me if their dad approved of this venture, and I assured them that he supported me wholeheartedly. I could tell that they didn't completely believe me and suspected there was more to the story than I was telling them, but they didn't pursue it.

Dan was getting ready to graduate and Kent was a sophomore in college; both of them had flown the parsonage nest. I didn't say anything about moving out at this time. I would wait until I had a job offer somewhere and cross that bridge later. We had a wonderful weekend together, the three of us, doing the things that we had always enjoyed doing together – eating pizza, playing card games, and watching movies on TV.

This all sounds simple and scheming, which it was. I was operating on autopilot, looking out for myself for the first time in my life, and willing to do whatever I had to do in order to survive, both emotionally and physically.

After getting a negative result to STD tests that I had the week after my discovery of Chad's sexual activities, I breathed a little easier, at least from a health point of view. At that time, I never dreamed that my decision was going to take a turn that would make Chad look like an angel and me like a demon.

TRANSITIONS, ONCE AGAIN

I began dropping hints to the church members I knew that I was hoping to get a new job, one that was closer to my educational background than my current part-time job. With my degree in Sociology and my experience working in offices, I felt confident that something would come my way.

I started applying for positions in any areas I felt I was the least bit qualified, and started stashing every extra penny I could get my hands on. I made sure that Chad understood that he would help me out financially until I got on my feet and until our divorce was final. If he balked, all I had to do was threaten to go to the Clergy Superintendent and tell him the sorted story.

Chad was wedged between a rock and a hard place, and he knew it. He continued to beg me not to leave, but my course was set, and I knew that there was no way I could stay with him a minute longer than I had to.

By springtime, I had a job lined up as an executive assistant with the Georgia Department of Social Services. It was far enough from where we lived that my plan to rent an apartment made sense to the church members - at least nobody said anything to us about it. Lying again, I told people that I would be spending the weeknights at the apartment, and then come home to the parsonage every weekend. I found a furnished garage apartment in a nice neighborhood not far from my new job, rented it, and began moving some of my personal possessions to the new place.

Chad was pathetic. He continued begging me not to leave him alone. What was he going to do without me there to support him? I assured him that he would be fine, and in a moment of pure meanness, I told him he could always count on Joe or another of his "friends."

On a sunny May Saturday, I packed my car with the last of the things I thought I'd need for the time being, and backed out of the parsonage driveway. I'd arranged for Dan and Kent to meet me at my new apartment with something for dinner, probably pizzas, my comfort food of choice. Chad wasn't around to say good-bye to me, and I was glad that I didn't have to deal with his blubbering pleas. My new job was scheduled to begin the following Monday, and I was both excited and terrified. I thought about Chad being alone in the parsonage, but pushed the thought to the back of my mind as quickly as I could.

For the next two months, I was true to my word in returning home for weekends, putting on my happy face and pretending that nothing was wrong. Then I began skipping weekends, and by the end of summer, I wasn't going back at all.

In the meantime, some of the church members began questioning Chad, and he told them that he was filing for divorce. The rumors spread like wildfire around the church and beyond to other churches and people we knew. Everyone, as far as I knew, assumed that I was the one caught having an affair, and that was the reason I had moved out. Since I wasn't handy to defend myself, Chad let the rumors fly without doing anything to squelch them.

I decided to go ahead and take the heat - I really didn't have a choice - since I wasn't associated with the church any more, and didn't even attend services anywhere. I didn't know what Chad was telling his parishioners, but it didn't matter to me. I was still angry and bitter, and I had my own demons to exorcize. All I wanted was a bit of peace, and I found it in my little apartment and in my job.

My gift for Thanksgiving was a set of divorce papers to sign. Chad was true to his word in dividing our meager assets equally. Since we had no furniture, and he hadn't saved a penny during the whole time we were married, there wasn't much to split up between the two of us. He didn't seem to care what I took with me. He always thought I had too much "junk" in the parsonage. I was offered a cash settlement in lieu of half of his pension, which I took. He also took responsibility for the remainder of Kent's college expenses. And he got to keep his secret. I thought this was worth a lot more than my share of the china, crystal and silver, but I was satisfied. My birdcage door was finally open, and I flew out, junk and all, never to return.

The boys visited Chad on Christmas morning that year before coming to my apartment for Christmas dinner. They told me that he was doing OK, but missed me terribly. He had plans to go visit a friend later that day. I knew who he was going to see, but didn't say anything or ask any questions.

LIFE GOES ON – FOR SOME

The following June, Chad moved to a new church. He accepted an appointment at a smaller church in northwest Georgia. I think he wanted a church that was less demanding of his emotional time, and one where he wasn't as well known. I didn't keep up with him anymore, and was doing my best to build a life for myself and get myself on a good financial footing.

I was making new friends and having a social life, which was something I had missed out on for all those parsonage years. Both of my sons were now college graduates and heading out on their own adult lives and careers. I didn't see or hear from them as much as I would have liked, but I was filling my new life with new people and adventures.

I was also making plans to move. I had applied for a promotion with the state agency, which would place me in a satellite office in middle Georgia, where I would take on new administrative duties and even have a staff of my own. My degree in Sociology was finally paying off for me. I had already begun looking for a home to purchase, even though the promotion wouldn't be final for several months.

On a January afternoon, the year after Chad had moved, I was surprised when both Dan and Kent appeared at my office door.

"Mom," Dan took the lead. "We have some bad news to tell you." I sat back in my chair, took a deep breath, and waited for what they had to tell me.

"They found Dad this morning after he didn't show up at the church for a meeting," Kent said. "It was too late. He's gone, Mom."

"Do they know what happened," I asked, tears welling up in my eyes. Even after all I had been through, I felt suddenly empty.

"A heart attack, they think," Dan said. "At least that's what the policeman said after they got into the house. He said there was a broken coffee mug and spilled coffee on the floor next to Dad."

Holding back the tears, I grabbed my purse and jacket, and said, "Let's get out of here. I need to go home."

Dan drove my car and Kent followed in the one they had come in together. When we got inside my apartment home, I burst into tears, hugging both of my boys with all I was worth. I felt a huge black hole inside of me, even though Chad had been gone from my life for over two years. He had been such a huge part of my life for over 20 years, and nothing could take that away from me. Not even Joe.

What about Joe? Should he be told? Was it my obligation to do anything about this? Somehow, someway, the news would reach him. All I knew was that Chad was gone. The stress of all those years of hiding who he was and keeping secrets had taken its fatal toll. I hoped that the end had come quickly for him and that he was finally at peace.

Something healed in me that day. I let Chad go, at last, and let all of my bitterness drift heavenward with my wishes that he was at last who he was created to be.

I didn't go to his funeral. There were too many people who loved Chad dearly who also believed that I was the reason for our divorce and, inevitably, his death. I didn't want to face any of those people from my past. Dan and Kent didn't really like it, but they didn't try to force me to go with them. From what they told me, the church was filled to capacity - standing room only - with people who had been members of Chad's churches over the years. Many of his former parishioners had offered warm memories of him and his ministry. They told me that it had been a very nice service.

A month after Chad's death, the boys were at my home having dinner with me. They both seemed on edge, and I knew that there was something they needed to talk to me about.

This time, Kent took the lead. "Mom, you need to tell us the truth about you and Dad. We know that the rumors weren't true about you, but we knew something must have happened to cause you to move out the way you did."

"Dad was gay, wasn't he?" Dan blurted out. "That was what it was all about, wasn't it?"

I sighed, the truth finally out, the secret - or part of it - now out in the open. Slowly, deliberately, I told the story, doing my best not to make Chad look like a horrible person, but one who was tormented by something that he didn't understand and couldn't change, no matter how hard he tried.

But I couldn't bring myself to tell my sons my beliefs that Chad was probably bisexual, and possibly had some form of sexual addiction. I was not a psychologist, and only knew what I remembered from an *Abnormal Psychology* class I had taken in college. I certainly was not an expert on the subject. Since we had never gone to counseling, I only had my experiences with Chad to fall back on. I left out the sexual stuff that I now recognized as Chad's attempt to be heterosexual and "normal."

I also left out what I had figured out about his relationship with his parents, mainly his father, and his being such a disappointment to his dad. I didn't want to have any more secrets, but I felt that there were some things that just weren't necessary to tell at the time. All would come out later if needed. Some things should be left untold for the time being.

"Why did you let people think and say those awful things about you, Mom?" Dan asked.

I sighed again, searching for the right words. "When I found out about your father, I felt empty, totally empty, and betrayed. But he was so pitiful and afraid, I just couldn't bring myself to tear everything from him. He was an excellent preacher and pastor, and being a minister was all he ever wanted to be. I promised to keep his secret, because I felt like it was his and not mine. It was up to him to decide what to do with it."

I paused, collected my thoughts and concluded, "What people thought about me didn't matter. I was leaving and wouldn't ever be back. I didn't anticipate the viciousness of the rumor mill at the time, or I might have done things differently. But that is now all water under the bridge, and I have no control over what people have said or thought. Your dad is gone, and our lives go on."

Indeed, life does go on. Finally telling my sons the truth lifted a huge burden from my heart. I mourned Chad's death — we had a lifetime together that couldn't and shouldn't be erased. I also had two grown sons who were the light of my life. During all of those years I had become a strong person, had found my voice, and had accomplished a great deal in spite of the obstacles I had to overcome. I was determined to rid myself of any lingering bitterness, which seemed to me to be a huge waste of energy, and to look forward. My last act of moving on with my life was to take back my maiden name,

McDougall. I didn't want to carry Chad's name any longer, and now that my sons were grown, I felt no need to do so.

It was soon time to move. With my new job and promotion coming up, I found a house to buy near the little town of Wellspring, ten miles from my new office. It was nothing fancy, a plain frame bungalow that reminded me of something out of a Disney cartoon movie, sitting on two acres of land. The price was right, so I bought it. With the boys' help, we packed up all of my belongings from my little apartment in Atlanta into Dan's pick-up truck and Kent's and my cars and set out for my new adventure.

LIFE THROWS CURVES, BUT ALSO DELIVERS GIFTS

I settled into my new home and office as a single woman. Hardly anyone I met in Wellspring or at my new office knew that I had been a minister's wife, and those who did never mentioned it to me. I kept my past tucked closely to me and when asked about my marital status, I simply stated that I was divorced and my ex-husband was now dead. Sometimes I would tell a gentle fib if someone pried into my husband's occupation.

I would smile and say, "He was in the insurance business." If I had to elaborate, I'd add, "Life insurance."

Here I was in my late-forties, finally supporting myself, living my life on my own terms. I took to my new environment like a duck takes to water. I had taken Virginia Woolf's book *A Room of One's Own* to heart, and from reading it I yearned for a room of my own. I now had it in the form of my charming little house, and I was as happy as a clam. I lived a simple life – for a couple of years I slept on a day bed which doubled as a couch, and the only comfortable chair in my home was the rocking chair that Chad had given me years before.

Little by little, I furnished my new home with odds and ends. It became a joke with me whenever someone would ask me how I decorated my cozy little house, I'd smile and say, "Contemporary Divorce."

Dan and Kent worried about me at first, but they soon came to see that I could take care of myself, and with each challenge I met I was becoming a stronger and more independent woman. My voice was becoming more unique, and I had shed the shroud of invisibility. They were as proud of me as I was of myself.

I had to decide what to do about religion, church, guilt, and my faith.

I carried a huge sense of guilt that I had somehow let God down in not living up to whatever it was that I was supposed to do and be as a minister's wife. At times I also felt like I was the reason that Chad had died. If I had stayed with him and continued to support him in his ministry, he could continue living his private life, being a good pastor, and still maintaining his family man image. Maybe he wouldn't have had that heart attack and died. But then I'd think about myself and ponder what might have happened to me had I stayed.

During the last year of our marriage I was haunted with suspicions about him, and felt battered from his paranoia and accusations. Thinking more and more about it, I realized that we were a time bomb waiting to explode, and the damage could have been extensive. As it turned out, the way I exited quietly and kept his secret may have been the best diffusion of the fuse that would have ignited a huge explosion. The ending wasn't happy, but it wasn't as horrible as it could have been.

I also released the guilt I'd carried all the years believing I had somehow killed my firstborn son. I had never forgiven myself for whatever sin I must have committed to cause the miscarriage. Chad hadn't been any help, either. Whenever I'd attempt to unburden myself, he's stop me with, "It was God's will, Fran. You mustn't question God." When I was finally able to face God and indeed question him, I was finally freed from this horrible weight on my soul. I had been given two beautiful sons – my first grace gifts from God.

I felt that my church and religion had let me down. The Southern Evangelical Church threw me out with the bathwater when Chad filed for divorce. I received several nasty letters and phone calls from church members and from Chad's minister friends berating me for walking out on him and for deserting my home, my family, and the church. I often thought about Lori, and understood why she chose to simply disappear from everything and everyone she had known who was connected with the church. I sometimes thought if I should have done the same thing. Thankfully, after Chad died, all of this ended, and after taking back my maiden name, my identity as his wife was buried with him. The church had no hold over me any longer.

My faith was another matter. If it weren't for a deep-rooted faith that had been with me since childhood, I don't think I could have weathered this storm. The music of the church was my salvation, and it was through music that my soul was finally stilled.

I began attending a Methodist church, similar to the one from my childhood, and I would sit in my spot on the last pew, tears running down my cheeks as I listened to the organ music and let it wash over me, soothing my damaged spirit. I also carried on spirited arguments with God, lashing out at him and sending my anger heavenward.

Once I moved to Wellspring, I could go for long walks or sit quietly on my porch, absorbing the beauty of each day, and letting God find his way into my heart again. I continued to have questions and doubts, but I reasoned that God never tired of them, and didn't hold it against me for asking him the same questions over and over again.

Through my work in social services, I found my passion in helping those in greater need than mine to find their way in life and get back on their feet. My work fulfilled my yearning to do something meaningful with my life. Slowly, I healed and, slowly, I discovered a new faith that I could call my own and one that I could live.

Now that the church no longer held me in her grasp, I didn't feel guilty if I missed a Sunday, or two, or three. I remained drawn toward the church, and joined the local Methodist Church after I had been in Wellspring for several years. But I had discovered that my faith and my belief in God wasn't tied up in the church, and I didn't need it to feed my soul.

From all of this I began recognizing other grace gifts in my life. While my years as a minister's wife were far from perfect, often sending me off in despair over what I was doing and where I was going in my life, there were so many gifts of grace to help me grow strong and to smooth out the difficult paths.

It was through grace that I flourished while swimming in a fishbowl or confined to a birdcage, and it was through grace that I was able to bloom where I was planted, all the while finding my own voice and escaping from the invisibility of living in Chad's shadow. All of those years prepared me for my new life in Wellspring. And once on my own, I accepted God's grace with a deep gratitude, and became more in tune with the spiritual nature of God.

The years that followed, working on my career and nurturing my home, were good ones. As with anyone, the good times were interspersed with challenging and trying moments, but with my newfound inner strength, I crossed those bridges and forded those streams reaching the other side intact.

I made some wonderful new friends, and caught up with some old ones, reconnecting with a few childhood friends. I could count on the fingers of one hand the number of former church members who cared enough to keep up with me, mostly through newsy Christmas letters.

My biggest disappointment was that Lori didn't want to stay in touch with me, but I respected her wishes, let her go, and wished her Godspeed in her life. My life was wrapped up in my two acres, my little home, my work, and my sons. Dan and Kent had grown into wonderful men, and I was very proud of their accomplishments. I vowed not to smother love them, and let them live their lives without my constant checking up on them, even though I prayed each day for many years that they would each find someone special to share their lives with. I finally came to my senses, quit praying about this and handed them over to God. They both were good sons, were there if I needed them, and in turn let me live my own life without hovering over me.

It turned out to be a very good arrangement for the three of us. I knew in looking back over my life that I had done something good in bringing up my two boys.

THE BIGGEST DISCOVERY OF ALL

The year that I turned 58 was also the year of my high school 40-year reunion. I was unable to attend due to a conflict associated with my job, but I filled out the form that was sent out to everyone from my class, which included a brief biography - I left out the preacher's wife years - and contact information. There was nothing about the reunion that drew me toward it, and I was inwardly glad that the date coincided with our department's annual employee retreat.

The day came and went without my awareness of it more than a passing thought that it was also occurring while I was in the North Georgia mountains with my co-workers. Two weeks later when I received the reunion yearbook in the mail with everyone's personal information neatly printed in alphabetical order, I glanced at it briefly and set it on my coffee table to look at when I had some spare time.

One evening shortly after this, my phone rang. When I answered, a man's voice said, "I am looking for Frances McDougall who graduated from North Point High School. Have I reached the right person?"

"Yes, this is Fran," I answered hesitantly. "Who is this?"

"I don't know if you'll remember me," the voice said. "This is Jeff Johnson. We haven't talked for, what? Thirty years?"

Oh my God! Talk about a blast from the past. I hadn't thought about Jeff in decades. My heart began to pound, remembering the last time I had seen him, at our 10 year reunion. With a quiver in my voice I said, "Jeff Johnson! Of course I remember you! How are you, and where are you?"

"I'm doing fine, Fran," he answered. "I just received our reunion book and looked you up, hoping you had sent in info about yourself." There was a slight hesitation in his voice. "I was wondering if I could come to visit you."

"Of course you can, Jeff," I replied. "Where are you living now?"

"Right now I am in Atlanta, but I don't know if I'll be staying here. I'm sort of at loose ends since I retired."

We talked for a few more minutes and decided on a date for him to come to see me, the following Saturday afternoon. Wellspring is about 80 miles from

Atlanta, so it wouldn't be much of a trip for him to make.

As I hung up the phone, I was experiencing a flutter in my stomach that I hadn't felt since I was 20 years old. I couldn't wait for Saturday to get here.

HERE'S TO HAPPY BEGINNINGS

So, I sit on my porch as I do on almost every pleasant afternoon, drinking my glass of wine, swinging and watching the clouds float across the azure sky. As I've thought about my life and the paths I've taken to reach this place - to this day - I marvel at my journey.

I am listening for the sound of Jeff's truck and looking for its trail of dust to make an appearance on my dirt road. Maggie is watching for him, too, and she'll let me know with a friendly bark and wagging tail that he has turned onto our road before I ever see his truck. Martin and Coretta have settled down for a nap on the welcome mat, oblivious that we'll soon have company. When Jeff gets here, they will probably race indoors and head for the rafters. It's been seven years since his phone call. He'll be here for dinner, and then will stay the night with me.

The Saturday that Jeff came to visit me is a day that I hope I never get too old or senile to forget. In many ways, I look back at that afternoon as the first day of the rest of my life. I watched for him to arrive the same as I am doing today, except on that day the butterflies in my stomach were flying around like crazy, knocking into one another and making me quite swimmy-headed. I didn't know what to expect, but I was looking forward to seeing Jeff more than anything in quite a long time.

I recognized him the instant he opened his truck door and stepped out. A little older, a lot grayer, but still slender and handsome. When he smiled, I recognized the eighteen-year-old Jeff behind the creased and lined face, who comforted me over my break-up with Kyle and who sang beside me in our school's production of *South Pacific*. He bounded up the steps to my porch and gave me a huge bear hug and a kiss on the cheek. I melted, electricity coursing through me, as I felt his arms around me and the touch of his lips on my face. I didn't believe that a postmenopausal woman could still have those kinds of feelings.

As we drew apart, he held me at arms' length, studying my face while I did the same with his. All he said was, "Fran, it's been 'way too long."

I answered, "I'm so glad that you're here."

And so it began, the love affair of my life.

It took quite awhile for us to share our individual histories with each other. I learned that after two tours in Vietnam, Jeff spent a couple of years moving from city to city on his motorcycle, trying to find a place to settle down. He finally landed in Nashville,

Tennessee, where he could nurture his love of music and play his guitar and sing with small country music bands around town. Knowing that he probably wouldn't ever become a famous musician, he took up the carpentry trade and became a master carpenter. It was a good occupation for him, because he suffered from post-traumatic-stress syndrome from the horrors he experienced in Vietnam, and as a result had a difficult time with authority figures and working in a structured or enclosed environment, such as an office setting with people to tell him what to do. As a carpenter, he was able to be his own boss and control his schedule and the jobs he wanted to undertake.

He finally retired at age 58, drawing on his veteran's disability and his savings. He moved to Atlanta, hoping to find some part-time work to supplement his income and to have a change of view. He had been married once, briefly, but never had any children, so he had the freedom to go wherever he wanted. When he made the move, he didn't know that I was as close by as I was.

I gave him the *CliffNotes* version of my life that day. Over time, he has learned more about my life, as I have his. We have become an item among my family members. Everyone likes Jeff, and hope that we'll get married. I don't think we will, and I don't think we need to.

Jeff made the move to Wellspring a few months later. He doesn't live with me, and we both like it this way. He bought a small house on the other side of town in a neat little subdivision. He has set up a carpentry shop in his garage, and he designs and builds custom furniture made from high quality wood. He is becoming well-known in the area for his craftsmanship. You can see some of his creations in the Wellspring Furniture Store, where they are sold on consignment. He also plays his guitar in a local country music band, which brings in a small income and a lot of enjoyment for him.

I never knew that sex could be as lovely as it is with Jeff, or that I would be enjoying it at my advanced age. And normal – none of the weirdness that I endured with Chad. I have found that I anticipate lovemaking with Jeff, and if he should wake me up in the middle of the night (which he doesn't), I'd be eager and ready to join him in intimacy. Since we are older than the average bear now, intimate moments aren't as frequent as when we were younger, but we've found that intimacy can be wrapped in many enjoyable packages.

Now that I am retired, as well, Jeff and I are together as much as either of us wants to be. We enjoy each other's company and respect each other's privacy. On warm evenings he'll get out his old guitar, which is with him all the time, and we'll sing together out on my porch, often songs from *South Pacific* and other Broadway shows from our day. It's a good thing we don't have any close neighbors, because I'm sure it's sometimes painful to the ears. Maggie is a good barometer of the quality of our voices, as she will either attempt to out-sing us, or simply leave to go to her cozy bed in my bedroom.

Jeff also helps me around my property when I need a strong back to plow my garden or keep my property from becoming overrun with briars and brambles. We each relish our individual space, however, and at this time have no plans to combine our resources and live together. Who knows what we'll do in the future. For now, we are happy.

I sit and swing, content at last and satisfied that I've found my unique place in God's world. I know that I am in the spot where I am supposed to be. Finally free from the fishbowl and the birdcage, I am solidly planted in the red Georgia clay here in Wellspring.

And I am blooming.

THE END

ABOUT THE AUTHOR

Jennie Campbell lives in Monroe, Georgia, with her dog and constant companion, Sunshine. When not writing, she enjoys gardening, making jellies and preserves, and going on long walks. Her blog, *A Collection of Brand New Days*, can be found at: www.jennielousdays.wordpress.com.

43931364R00160

Made in the USA
Lexington, KY
23 August 2015